That light touch that seemed perilously close to a caress made Tati shiver while her skin broke out in goose bumps of awareness. "You don't understand…"

"The only thing I understand right now is that I want you."

"Me? You want…*me*?" Tati almost whispered.

"Why wouldn't I want you?" Saif turned the question back on her in equal surprise. "You are a remarkable beauty."

That was a heady compliment for a woman who had never been called beautiful in her entire life, who was always in the shadows, either unnoticed or passed over or summarily dismissed as being unimportant. Tati stared at him in astonishment, and she was so blasted grateful for that tribute that she stretched up and kissed his cheek in reward.

As her breasts momentarily pressed into his chest and the intoxicating scent of her engulfed him, the soft invitation of her lips on his skin burned through Saif's self-discipline like a fiery brand and destroyed it. Without any hesitation, he closed her slight body into the circle of his arms and brought his mouth crashing down on hers with a hunger he couldn't even attempt to control.

Heirs for Royal Brothers

When one night with a prince has life-changing consequences!

Royal half brothers Prince Saif Basara of Alharia and Prince Angelino Diamandis of Themos are both scarred by the dramatic circumstances of their births. Their upbringings might have been very different, but they are united in one key goal—to never fall in love!

But fate has other plans when the guarded brothers meet their matches in Tatiana Hamilton and Gabriella Knox. And only a royal wedding will do when there are royal heirs involved!

Read Saif and Tatiana's story in
Cinderella's Desert Baby Bombshell

Available now!

Read Angelino and Gabriella's story in
Her Best Kept Royal Secret

Coming soon!

Lynne Graham

CINDERELLA'S DESERT BABY BOMBSHELL

HARLEQUIN®
PRESENTS®

Recycling programs for this product may not exist in your area.

ISBN-13: 978-1-335-56794-9

Cinderella's Desert Baby Bombshell

Copyright © 2021 by Lynne Graham

All rights reserved. No part of this book may be used or reproduced in any manner whatsoever without written permission except in the case of brief quotations embodied in critical articles and reviews.

This is a work of fiction. Names, characters, places and incidents are either the product of the author's imagination or are used fictitiously. Any resemblance to actual persons, living or dead, businesses, companies, events or locales is entirely coincidental.

This edition published by arrangement with Harlequin Books S.A.

For questions and comments about the quality of this book, please contact us at CustomerService@Harlequin.com.

Harlequin Enterprises ULC
22 Adelaide St. West, 40th Floor
Toronto, Ontario M5H 4E3, Canada
www.Harlequin.com

Printed in U.S.A.

Lynne Graham was born in Northern Ireland and has been a keen romance reader since her teens. She is very happily married to an understanding husband who has learned to cook since she started to write! Her five children keep her on her toes. She has a very large dog who knocks everything over, a very small terrier who barks a lot and two cats. When time allows, Lynne is a keen gardener.

Books by Lynne Graham

Harlequin Presents

Indian Prince's Hidden Son
The Greek's Convenient Cinderella
The Ring the Spaniard Gave Her

Cinderella Brides for Billionaires

Cinderella's Royal Secret
The Italian in Need of an Heir

Innocent Christmas Brides

A Baby on the Greek's Doorstep
Christmas Babies for the Italian

Passion in Paradise

The Innocent's Forgotten Wedding

Visit the Author Profile page
at Harlequin.com for more titles.

CHAPTER ONE

THE HEIR TO the throne of the Middle Eastern kingdom of Alharia, Prince Saif Basara, frowned as his father's chief adviser, Dalil Khouri, knocked and entered his office with a charged air of importance and the solemn bearing of a man about to deliver vital information.

In recent years Saif had heard every possible story relating to his father's eccentric dictates and views. He was thirty years old, his difficult parent's successor, and the courtiers of his father's inner circle were now routinely playing a double game—nodding with false humility at his father's medieval dictums and then coming to Saif to complain and lament.

The Emir of Alharia was eighty-five years old and horrendously out of step with the modern world.

Of course, Saif's father, Feroz, had come to the throne in a very different age, a feudal ruler in an unstable era when a troubled country was overwhelmingly grateful to have a safe and steady monarch. Oil had then been discovered. Subsequently, the coffers

of Alharia had overflowed and for decades everyone had been happy with that largesse. Unhappily
for Feroz, the desire for democratic government had
eventually blossomed in his people, as well as the
wish to modify cultural rules with an easier and more
contemporary way of life. He, however, remained
rigidly opposed to change of any kind.

'You are to be married!' Dalil announced with so
much throbbing drama that Saif very nearly laughed
until he registered that the older man was deadly
serious.

Married? Saif stiffened in surprise, well aware
that only his father's misogyny had allowed him to
remain single for longer than most sons in his position. After four failed marriages in succession, Feroz
had become deeply distrustful of women. His final
wife, Saif's mother, had inflicted the deepest wound
of all. An Arabian princess of irreproachable lineage,
she had, nonetheless, abandoned both infant son and
elderly husband to run away with another man. That
she had then married that man and become joint ruler
of another small country and thereafter *thrived* in
tabloid newspaper photographs enraptured with her
beauty had definitely been salt rubbed in an open
wound.

'Married to a very *bad* choice of a woman,' Dalil
completed with regret, mopping his perspiring brow
with an immaculate linen handkerchief. 'The Emir
has turned his back on all the many respectable pos-

sibilities both in Alharia and amongst our neighbours' families and has picked a foreigner.'

'A foreigner,' Saif repeated in wonderment. 'How
is that possible?'

'This woman is the granddaughter of your father's
late English friend, Rodney Hamilton.'

As a young man, the Emir had undergone a few
months of military training at Sandhurst in England,
where he had formed an unbreakable friendship with
a British army officer. For years, the two men had
exchanged letters and at least once there had been a
visit. Saif dimly recalled a whiny, weepy little girl
with blond pigtails appearing in his nursery. His future bride? Was that even possible?

Dalil dug out the mobile phone he kept carefully
hidden from the Emir, to whom mobile phones were
an abomination. He flicked through photos and
handed it to Saif, saying, 'At least she is a beauty.'

Saif noted that his father's adviser took it for
granted that he would accept an arranged marriage
with a stranger, and he swallowed hard, shocked by
the apparent belief that he was required to make that
sacrifice. He stared down unimpressed at a laughing, slender blonde in an evening gown. She looked
frivolous and wholly unsuited to the life that he led.
'What do you know about her?' he prompted.

'Tatiana Hamilton is a socialite, an extravagant
party girl...not at all the kind of wife you would wish
for, but in time...' Dalil hesitated to avoid referring

to the reality that the Emir's failing health would not conserve the ruler for ever. 'Obviously, you would divorce her.'

'It is possible that I will refuse this proposition,' Saif confessed tautly.

'You *can't*…it could kill your father to go into one of his rages now!' Dalil protested in consternation. 'Forgive me for speaking so bluntly, but you do not want that on your conscience.'

Saif breathed in slow and deep as he faced the truth that he was trapped. He banked down his anger with the ease of long practice, for he had grown up in a world in which personal choice about anything was a rare gift. He had been raised to be a dutiful son and, now that his parent was weak and ailing, it was a huge challenge to break that conditioning. It didn't help that he also understood that it would be very painful for his traditional parent to be confronted by a defiant son. Arranged marriages might have been out of fashion for decades in Alharia but, at heart, the Emir was a caring father and Saif was not cruel. He was also very conscious that he was indebted to his father for the loving care he had practised in an effort to ensure that his son was less damaged by his mother's abandonment.

Consequently, he would wed a stranger, he acknowledged, bitterness darkening his stunning green eyes.

'Why would a spoilt English socialite want to marry me and come out here?' he demanded of the older man in sudden incomprehension. 'For a title? Surely not?'

A look of distaste stamped Dalil's wrinkled face. 'For the money, Your Royal Highness. For the lavish dowry your father is prepared to pay her family,' he replied in a tone of repugnance. 'They will be greatly enriched by this marriage and that is why you will wish to divorce her as soon as possible.'

Saif was aghast at that statement. It gave him the worst possible impression of his future bride and filled him with revulsion. He knew that he would find it very hard to pretend any kind of acceptance of such an unprincipled woman…

'George has just asked me to marry him!' Ana carolled, practically dancing out of the bathroom where she had been talking on the phone to her ex-boyfriend. 'Isn't that typical of a man? It took me to come to Alharia and be on the very brink of marrying another man to get George to the point!'

'Well, it's a bit foolish, him asking you this late in the day,' Tati opined with innate practicality as she studied her beautiful and lively cousin with sympathetic blue eyes. 'I mean, we're here in the *royal* palace and you're committed now. The preparations for the wedding are starting in less than an hour.'

'Oh, I'm not going through with this stupid wedding now—not if George wants me to marry him instead!' Ana declared with sunny conviction.

'George has already booked me on a flight home. He's planning to pick me up at the airport and whisk me away for a beach wedding somewhere.'

'But your parents…the money.'

'Why should I have to marry some rich foreign royal because my father's in debt to his eyeballs?' Ana interrupted with unconcealed resentment.

Tati winced at that piece of plain speaking. 'Well, I didn't think you should have to either, but you did *agree* to do it and if you back out now, it'll plunge us all into a nightmare. Your father will go spare!'

'Yes, but that's where *you* are going to *help* me play for time and ensure that I can get back out of this wretched country!' her cousin told her without hesitation.

'Me? How can I help?' Tati argued in bewilderment, because she was the most powerless member of the Hamilton family, the proverbial poor relation often treated as little more than a servant by Ana's parents.

'Because *you* can go through these silly bridal preparations pretending to be me, so that nobody will know that the bride has scarpered until it's too late. I mean, in a place as backward as this, they might try to *stop* me leaving at the airport if they find out beforehand! I bet it's a serious crime to jilt the heir to the throne at the altar!' Ana exclaimed with a melodramatic roll of her big brown eyes. 'But, luckily, no member of the groom's family has even seen me yet and Mum's certainly not going to be getting involved with these Alharian wedding rituals, so the parents won't find out either until the very last minute, by which time I'll be safely airborne!'

Tati dragged in a ragged breath as her cousin completed that confident little speech. 'Are you sure this isn't an attack of cold feet?' she pressed.

'You know I'm in love with George and I have been…*for ever*!' her cousin stressed with strong feeling. 'Didn't you hear me, Tati? George has finally proposed and I'm going home to him!'

Tati resisted the urge to remind her cousin how many other men she had been wildly in love with in recent years. Ana's affections were unreliable and only a month earlier she had claimed to be excitedly looking forward to her wedding in Alharia. Back then, Ana had been as delighted as her parents at the prospect of no longer being short of cash, but of course, that angle would no longer matter to her, Tati conceded ruefully, because George Davis-Appleton was a wealthy man.

'I can understand that you want to do that.' Tati sighed. 'But I don't think I want to get involved in the fallout. Your parents will be furious with me.'

'Oh, don't be such a wet blanket, Tati! You're *still* family,' Ana declared, impervious as always to her cousin's low standing in that sacrosanct circle. 'Mum and Dad will get over their disappointment and they'll just have to ask the bank for a loan instead.'

'Your father said that he'd been refused a loan,' Tati reminded her gently.

'Oh, if only Granny Milly was still alive…she would have helped!' Ana lamented. 'But it's not my problem…it's Dad's.'

Tati said nothing, only reflecting that their late and much-missed Russian grandmother had had little time for her son Rupert's extravagant lifestyle. Milly Tatiana Hamilton, after whom both girls had been named, had controlled the only real money in her family for many years. Tati had been surprised at her uncle getting into debt again because she had assumed that he had inherited a sizeable amount after his mother's death.

'Sadly, she's gone.' Tati sighed heavily.

She did not, of course, point out that she had a vested interest in her aunt and uncle remaining financially afloat because she felt that that would be utterly unfair to Ana. She could hardly expect her cousin to go through with a marriage that would be abhorrent to her simply for Tati's benefit. In any case, Ana appeared to have no idea that her father paid for his sister Mariana's care in her nursing home. Tati's mother, Mariana, had lived there since her daughter was a teenager, having contracted early onset dementia.

'So, will you do it?' the beautiful blonde demanded expectantly.

Tati flinched because she knew that she shouldn't risk angering her aunt and uncle lest they withdraw their financial support from her mother, but at the same time, she was as close to Ana as a sister. Ana was only two years older than Tati's almost twenty-two years. The pair of them had grown up on the same country estate and had attended the same schools. Regardless of how different in personality the two women were, Tati loved her cousin. Selfish and spoilt Ana might occasionally be, but Tati was accustomed to looking after Ana as though she were a young and vulnerable sister because Ana was not the sharpest tool in the box.

The whole 'marrying a foreign prince sight unseen to gain a fat dowry' scenario had never struck sensible Tati as anything but ludicrous. Naturally, her cousin should have had the sense to refuse to marry Prince Saif from the start because Ana was not the self-sacrificing type. But at first, Ana had seen herself as a heroine coming to the aid of her family. Furthermore, the tantalising prospect of increased wealth and status had soothed an ego crushed by George's refusal to commit to a future with her. Sadly, now that reality had set in, Ana was ready to run for the hills.

For a split second, Tati felt rather sorry for the bridegroom, whoever he might be, for he had no presence whatsoever on social media. Alharia seemed to be decades behind in the technology stakes—decades behind in most things, if she was honest, Tati had reflected after their drive through the desert wastes to the remote palace, which was an ancient fortress with mainly Victorian furnishings.

'All that money and no idea how to spend it or what to spend it on,' her aunt Elizabeth had bemoaned in envious anguish, soon after their arrival. And it was true: the Basara royal family might be oil billionaires, but there was little visible sign of that tremendous wealth.

Ana had met someone who had sworn blind that Prince Saif was 'absolutely gorgeous' but, as even Ana had said, how much faith could she place in that when people tended to be more generous when it came to describing rich, titled young men? Even if the poor chap were as ugly as sin, most would find something positive to say about him.

Tati knew all about that approach and the accompanying unkind comparisons, having grown up labelled a plain Jane beside her much prettier and thinner cousin. Of course, Tati was the family 'mistake' being illegitimate, something which might not matter to others, but which had seriously mattered to the uptight Hamilton family and had embarrassed them.

Both girls were blonde, but Tati had blue eyes and Ana had brown and Ana was a tall, slim beauty while Tati rejoiced rather more simply in good skin, a mane of healthy hair and curves. Well, she had never exactly *rejoiced* in her body, she conceded ruefully, particularly not after her only serious boyfriend had taken one look at her cousin and had fallen in love with her to the extent that he had made an embarrassing nuisance of himself, even though Ana had not had the smallest interest in him.

'Have you even thought of how you're going to get back to the airport?' Tati asked her cousin when she returned to the bedroom they were sharing.

'Already sorted,' Ana said smugly. 'You don't need the lingo to get by here. I flashed the cash, pointed to a car and it's downstairs waiting for me already.'

'Oh…' Tati whispered in shock as she watched her cousin scooping up her belongings and cramming them back into the suitcase she had refused to allow the maid to unpack. 'You're definitely doing this, then?'

'Of course, I am.'

'Don't you think it would be better to face the music and tell your parents that you're leaving?' Tati pressed hopefully.

'Are you joking?' Ana exclaimed. 'Have you any idea of the fuss they would make and how bad they would make me feel?'

Tati nodded in silence because, of course, she knew.

'Well, I'm not putting myself through that for

anybody!' Ana asserted. 'Now, you be careful. Don't let them realise that you're not the bride for a few hours…that's all I'm asking you to do, no big deal, Tati! Come on, give me a hug and wish me well with George!'

Tati rose stiffly and hugged her, because she knew how headstrong Ana was and that nothing short of a nuclear bomb would alter her plans once she had made her mind up. 'Be happy, Ana,' she urged with damp eyes and a sense of dread she couldn't shake.

Tati hated it when people got angry and started shouting and she knew that the moment her aunt and uncle realised that their daughter had departed there would be a huge scene and furious raised voices. They would blame *her* for not telling them in advance. At the same time, though, she understood her cousin's fears. Ana's parents were so set on the marriage taking place that they were quite capable of following her to the airport and trying to force her to return to the palace. How could she subject Ana to that situation when she no longer wanted to marry the wretched man? After all, nobody should be forced to marry anyone they didn't want to marry.

Ana departed with the utmost casualness, a gormless servant even carting her luggage for her without a clue that he was assisting the Prince's bride to stage a vanishing act. Tati sat on the edge of a seat in the corner of the bedroom, panicking at the very thought of allowing people to credit that she was her cousin and the bride-to-be. She supposed that that meant she was a coward and she felt ashamed of herself for being so weak. Deception of any kind was usually a complete no-no for Tati, whose birth father had gone to prison for financial fraud. Her mother, Mariana, ashamed of the character of the man who had fathered her daughter, had raised her to be honest and decent in all situations. And what was she doing now?

While Tati was struggling with her loyalty to her cousin, her anxiety about her mother's continuing care and her troubled conscience, someone knocked on the door and entered, a brightly smiling young woman, who greeted her warmly in English. 'Ta- tiana? I am the Prince's cousin, Daliya. I am a stu- dent in England, and I have been asked to act as your interpreter.'

'Everyone calls me Tati,' Tati told her appre- hensively, thinking how silly it was that she didn't even have to lie about her name because she and her cousin were both officially Tatiana Hamilton, thanks to her rebellious mother's obstinacy. Tati's mother and uncle had never got along as siblings. When Mariana's brother, Rupert, had named his child after his mother, his sister had seen no reason why he should claim that privilege and she should not. Of course, back then, her mother could never have foreseen that she would end up living back at her birthplace and that there would be two little girls rejoicing in the same name.

'I am sure you are wondering about the importance my people put on the bridal preparations,' Daliya assumed. 'Let me explain. This is not typical of weddings in Alharia because it is no longer fashionable. But you are different because this is a *royal* wedding. All the women who will attend you here today consider this a great honour. Most of them are from the older generation and this is how they demonstrate their respect, loyalty and love for the Basara family and the throne.'

'I shall feel privileged,' Tati squeezed out between clenched teeth, the guilt of being an impostor on such a solemn occasion cutting her deep. The pretty brunette's explanation had made her want to die of shame where she sat. The very least she could do was be polite and respectful…until the dreadful moment when people realised that she was *not* the right Tatiana Hamilton. Inwardly she was already recoiling in horror from the thought of that dramatic unveiling.

'All the same, I'm sure the unfamiliar will feel strange, and it may possibly intrude on your privacy to accept these diverse customs,' Daliya suggested, her intelligent brown eyes locked to Tati's face. 'You are very pale. Are you feeling all right? Is it the heat?'

'Oh, it's just nerves!' Tati exclaimed shakily as the other woman showed her out of the room and down a corridor. 'I'm very robust in the health stakes.'

Daliya laughed. 'The elderly women obsessed with your fertility will be delighted to hear that.'

'My f-fertility?' Tati stammered helplessly in her incomprehension.

'Of course. Some day you will be a queen and the natural hope is that you will provide the next generation to the throne.' Daliya frowned in surprise as Tati stumbled in receipt of that explanation.

For a split second, Tati had almost divulged the truth that she was not the right Tatiana, because it seemed so wrong to deceive people at such an important event. But they were already entering a very large room crammed with older women, some of whom wore the traditional dress but most of whom sported western fashion like her young companion.

Aware of being the centre of attention and ill accustomed to that sensation, Tati flushed just the way she used to do at school when the bullies had christened her 'Tatty Tato,' mocking her for her shabby second-hand uniforms and worn shoes. Her uncle's generosity in paying her school fees had not extended to such extras, and why should it have? she reflected, scolding herself for that moment of ingratitude. Tati had adored her loving mother growing up, but sometimes she had been embarrassed by her parent as well. Mariana Hamilton had never stood on her own feet and had never done anything other than casual work when it suited her. Relying on other people to pay her bills had come naturally to Tati's mother and that had made Tati both proud and independent. Or as proud and independent as one could be when forced to live in her uncle and aunt's country house and be at the family's beck and call while working for barely minimum wage.

All those thoughts teemed in Tati's busy brain while she calculated how many hours she would need to play the bridal role to allow Ana to make her getaway, and that introspection got her through the hideous public bathing rite she endured. Herbs and oils were stirred through a steaming bath and then she was wrapped in a modesty sheet, just as if she were entering a medieval convent, and settled into the water to have her hair washed. Keeping up an air of good cheer was hard. Daliya lightened the experience with explanations of the superstitions that had formed such rituals and cracking the occasional discreet joke.

'You are a very good sport,' Daliya whispered in quiet approbation. 'It is a good quality for a member of the royal family. I think all the women were afraid that you would refuse their attentions.'

Tati contrived to smile despite her discomfiture because she knew for a fact that nobody would have got to roll Ana in a sheet and steep her in a hot herbal bath that smelled like stewed weeds. Ana would have flatly refused any such ritual, too attached to her own regimented beauty routine and too afraid that her hair would be ruined. Unfamiliar with such routines, Tati had told herself that she was having a treat, a rather exotic treat admittedly but pretty much a treat for a young woman who generally washed, cut and styled her own hair. What little she earned only kept her in clothes and small gifts for her mother when she was able to visit her.

'You are very brave,' Daliya told her as her hair was being combed out.

'Why do you say that?'

'You are marrying a man you have never seen, never spoken to…or have you and the Prince met up in secret?' she prompted with unconcealed curiosity.

'No, we haven't. Isn't that the custom here? The sight-unseen thing?' Tati queried.

Daliya laughed out loud. 'Not in Alharia now for generations. We meet, we date. It is all very discreet, of course. Only the Emir follows old cultural traditions, but with the Prince you need have no fear of disappointment. Had His Royal Highness desired to marry any sooner, he would have been snatched up by any number of women.'

'Yes, I believe he's quite a catch,' Tati remarked politely.

'Saif is of a thoughtful, serious nature,' Daliya murmured quietly. 'He is very much admired in our country.'

Tati had to bite her tongue on the flood of curious questions that she wanted to fire at the brunette. It was none of her business. Even the Hamiltons knew next to nothing about the Crown Prince, for none of them had cared about the details. That the marriage should take place and the dowry be given had pretty much encompassed the extent of her relatives' interest and that awareness shamed Tati, because everything that her present companions took so seriously had been treated with scornful indifference by Ana and her parents.

At that point, Daliya contrived to persuade their chattering companions that the waxing technician could take Tati into the giant bathroom with its waiting treatment couch alone. Tati had never been so grateful for that small piece of mercy in the proceedings. Discovering that she was only an hour and a bit into the lengthy bridal preparations, she heaved a heavy sigh, knowing that her cousin needed longer to make good her escape from Alharia. She felt worse than ever about her deception.

After the waxing, the preparations moved on to a massage with scented oils. Her nails were painted and then henna patterns were drawn on her hands. Mentally exhausted, Tati drifted off into sleep and when she was wakened gently by Daliya, she sat up and was immediately served with a cold drink and a tasty little snack while all the women hummed some song around her. Her watch had disappeared, and she had no idea what time it was. Daliya was now telling her that she had to leave for a little while but would be back with her soon.

That announcement plunged Tati into an even deeper dilemma. She had originally planned to share her true status and the reality that the bride had fled with the chatty brunette, but she was painfully aware that Daliya had been very kind to her. As the only English speaker she might well receive considerable blame for not having registered the fact that the bride was not who she was supposed to be. After all, everybody was likely to get very worked up once the truth emerged. Tempers would be fraught, angry accusations would be made. Uneasily, Tati decided to wait for a less personal, more *official* messenger before confessing that she was a complete fraud in the bride stakes.

A long silk chemise garment was displayed for her benefit and it was evidently time for her to get dressed. She would be making her big reveal very soon, Tati acknowledged, sick at the prospect, her tummy hollowing out. But she had to be clothed to do anything, she reflected wretchedly, and she stood in silence while she was engulfed like an Egyptian mummy in layers of tunics and petticoats and her hair was combed out and a cosmetic technician every bit as slick as the type Ana used at home arrived to do her work. By the time Daliya reappeared beaming, Tati was ready to nibble her nails down to the quick, only she couldn't because they too had been embellished and she didn't want to offend anyone. And even that thought struck her as ridiculous, considering how offended everyone would be when the awful truth came out.

'It's time,' Daliya informed her cheerfully.

Tati feared she might throw up, so knotted were her insides by that stage, and the brunette's reappearance didn't help because she honestly didn't want to involve Daliya in her disaster. And it would *be* a disaster, she thought wretchedly. However, her aunt and uncle were the proper people to be told first that their daughter had fled. As they were to be witnesses to what Ana had described with a sniff of disappointment as a very *private* ceremony, she was sure to see Ana's parents very soon in the flesh.

A posse of chattering women walked her through the palace, down stone staircases, across inner courtyards, through endless halls and corridors until finally they reached a set of giant ornate double doors set with silver and glittering gems and guarded by two large men in traditional dress brandishing weapons.

'We must leave you here…but we will see you soon,' Daliya smilingly told her, exchanging a brief word with the guards that had them springing into action and throwing wide the double doors…

CHAPTER TWO

ONLY A SMALL number of people awaited the bride's arrival in the ancient splendour of that giant painted and gilded room, which was surrounded by elaborate carved archways and pillars. A regal elderly man was stationed by the side of another, taller figure shadowed by the archway below which he stood. Another pair of older men hovered beside a table, and across the room stood Rupert and Elizabeth Hamilton, Tati's uncle and aunt, glaringly out of place in their fashionable Western attire.

Rupert Hamilton frowned the instant he saw Tati and he strode forward. 'You're not supposed to be here for the ceremony. Where's Ana?'

Tati's mouth ran very dry. 'Gone,' she croaked.

'Gone?' the older man thundered. 'How can my daughter be gone? Gone where?'

Saif watched with keen eyes from the sidelines and wondered what was happening. Seemingly the bride had arrived, but her father was angry and that word, *gone*, was remarkably explanatory in such circumstances. Who on earth was the woman who had arrived in her place dressed as his bride? Saif almost laughed out loud with relief and amusement at the confirmation that the Basara family's bad luck with wives was continuing into his generation. Beside him, he could feel his father bristling with impatience, and he translated that single word for his benefit. 'The bride is gone,' he murmured in their own language. 'This is a different woman.'

'Gone to catch a flight back home. She'll be airborne by now,' Tati explained in a rush. 'She didn't want to go through with this.'

'You bitch! You helped her to run away!' her aunt Elizabeth shrilled at her in a tempestuous bout of annoyance, stalking across the room and lifting her hand as though to slap Tati.

'No…there will be no violence in the Emir's presence,' another voice intervened—male, accented, dark and deep in pitch.

Tati looked up in shock at the very tall young man who, for all his height and build, had approached so quietly and quickly that she hadn't heard him. He had caught her aunt's hand before it could connect with Tati's face, and he dropped the older woman's wrist again with a chilling air of disdain at such behaviour. And Tati's first thought was foolishly that Ana would be raging if she ever saw a photo of the bridegroom she had abandoned, because there were few women who appreciated a handsome man more than her cousin.

The big, well-built man towering over them, sheathed in an embroidered traditional tunic and trousers in opulent shades of brown silk worn with boots, was absolutely gorgeous. He had unruly black hair, eyes that were a startlingly unexpected and piercing green and lashes long enough to trip over, set deep below slashing ebony brows. He had skin the colour of creamy coffee whipped with cinnamon and stretched taut over spectacular bone structure, with a straight nose, a strong jawline and a wide sensual mouth. He was so good-looking that Tati's tongue was glued to the roof of her mouth and she simply stared at him as if he had suddenly materialised in front of her like an alien dropped from a spaceship.

'Be quiet, Elizabeth!' Rupert Hamilton snapped to silence his wife's ranting accusations. 'How long has it been since Ana left the palace?'

'It was hours ago,' Tati confirmed reluctantly.

The elderly man at the front of the room erupted into an angry speech in his own language. Saif shot a highly amused glance down at the bride who was not a bride. A sense of regained freedom and strong relief was now powering through him. She was tiny and she had huge blue eyes and a mass of wheat-blond hair that almost reached her waist…if she had a waist. The women had put so much clothing on the fake bride that she closely resembled a small moving mound of cloth. It was possible that she was rather round in shape but equally possible that she was built like a twig…and it didn't matter either way to him now, did it?

'And who are you?' he prompted with what he felt was excusable curiosity.

'Ana's cousin, Tati.'

'Which is a diminutive of?'

'Tatiana.'

'The same as the bride who is…*gone*?' Black lashes swooped down low over his glittering gaze and his mouth quirked. 'Is there a shortage of names in your family?' he enquired with complete insouciance, apparently untouched by the angry outbursts emanating from everyone else in the room.

A determined hand closed over her elbow, pulling her away from the silk-clad Prince. 'I want a word with you,' her uncle told her angrily. 'Here you are clearly *desperate* to take your cousin's place! That's why you helped her, isn't it? The temptation was too much for you. The thought of the clothes, the jewels and the holidays you'd be able to enjoy…the rich lifestyle that you've always dreamt of having and now, with Ana out of the way, it can *all* be yours!'

'Keep your voice down,' Tati pleaded with the older man because the Prince was only a few feet away from them.

She was absolutely horrified by her uncle's accusation that she had deliberately schemed to step into her cousin's shoes, that unspoken but deeply wounding suggestion that she must always have been envious of Ana and her superior financial prospects. 'Of course, I'm not trying to take Ana's place. Right now, you're upset—'

Dalil Khouri was endeavouring to explain to the enraged Emir that although a bride had arrived, she was not the chosen bride, she was a substitute even if she was another grandchild of the Emir's late friend. 'Well, then, let the ceremony proceed!' the old man commanded impatiently.

Saif, repelled by the brutal condemnation he had heard the uncle aim at his niece, made an attempt to reason with his exasperated parent, but his father could not move beyond the perceived affront of his precious only son and heir being jilted by his bride. The Emir could not accept that outrage. He felt it too deeply, chiming in as it did to his own unhappy past experiences with the opposite sex. 'I will not have my son left without a bride when the entire country knows he is to be wedded today,' he told his adviser with barely leashed anger. 'That is an insult we cannot accept. The other girl will do.'

Saif's brows shot up and he encountered a pleading look from Dalil, which almost made him roll his eyes. *'The other girl will do?'* Why not go out onto the street in Tijar, their capital city, and grab the first single woman they saw? Was he expected to marry *any* available woman? The volatile temperament that

Saif usually kept restrained was suddenly flaring with raw, angry disbelief. What kind of insanity was his father proposing now? If the bride had run off, goodbye and good riddance was Saif's response, as he was no keener on the marriage taking place than evidently she had been. But, tragically, his father was reacting with very real wrath to what he saw as a loss of face and an insult to the throne of Alharia.

Dalil aimed a powerless glance of regret in Saif's direction and crossed the room to speak to the Englishman. Saif twisted to attempt to reason with his father and then registered that the Emir was tottering and swaying where he stood. With a shout for assistance, he supported the frighteningly pale older man, and a guard came running with a chair.

'I am fine… I am good,' the Emir ground out between gritted teeth.

'Allow me to call Dr Abaza,' Saif urged.

'Unnecessary!' the Emir barked.

Dalil returned. 'It is your wish that the ceremony proceeds?' he prompted his ruler, while Saif thought in disgust of the mercenary young woman he was to be cursed with.

'Why else am I here?' the Emir demanded on a fresh burst of annoyance.

On the other side of the room Rupert Hamilton was cornering his niece. 'The Emir simply wants his son married off.'

'Why? What's wrong with him?' Tati questioned with a grimace.

'Well, you should be happy that all that needs to be altered on the paperwork is your birthdate,' her uncle told her, as though what he had suggested were a perfectly reasonable change. 'You will be marrying him in Ana's place.'

Tati stared up at the older man in disbelief. '*I'm* not willing to marry him!' she snapped half under her breath for emphasis.

Rupert Hamilton gave her an offensive smile. 'So you say,' he said, clearly unconvinced.

'I didn't seek this development,' Tati argued in a low, desperate undertone.

Her uncle shrugged. 'Then think of this as a long-overdue repayment for my family's generosity towards you and your idle, feckless mother,' he told her thinly. 'You owe us, Tati. You haven't put a bite of food in your mouth since you were born that hasn't come from this family. Now your mother's draining our resources like a leech…all these years in that overpriced nursing home—'

'She can't help that!' Tati exclaimed chokily, shaken at being confronted by his heartless resentment that her poor mother had not yet seen fit to die of the disease that had already robbed her of memory, physical health and enjoyment of life.

'If you want her to stay on there, you *will* marry the Prince,' her uncle told her callously. 'And if you don't marry him, she can go on welfare benefits and move to some council place where she'll be a damn sight less comfortable!'

'That's a horrible threat to make,' Tati whispered shakily. 'You can't still hate her that much. She's a frail shell of the woman she once was.'

'You made your choice. For whatever reasons, you *helped* Ana skip out on us...now *you* can pay the price!' her uncle slammed back at her bitterly.

For a split second, Tati lingered there, frozen to the spot as she stared into space. But she knew she didn't have a choice. The mother who had loved and appreciated her throughout her childhood deserved to be contented for what remained of her life. Dementia patients found any sort of change in their routines distressing and if Mariana Hamilton were moved to another home, she would very probably decline at an even faster rate. Tati neither liked nor respected her uncle, but she was willing to concede that perhaps he needed the dowry he was to receive from the marriage to help maintain her mother in her current home. He had called her mother a leech and apparently regarded his niece in the same light. That hurt, when she had spent the past six years industriously cleaning, cooking and fulfilling her relatives' every request to the best of her ability in repayment for her mother's care. Her work had begun while she was still at school and had eaten up every free hour, becoming a full-time job once she had completed sixth form.

'I'll do it,' she breathed stiffly. 'I don't have any other option.'

'Good.' Squaring his shoulders, her uncle walked over to the table and nodded at the older man. 'Well, let's get this over and done with.'

Barely able to credit that she was in such a position, Tati followed the older man across the room. The Prince approached the table but kept his distance, which suited her fine because she was already wondering what was amiss with him that his father could be so eager to marry him off that even a last-minute change of bride didn't dim his enthusiasm. Maybe he was a lecher and marriage was aimed at making him appear more respectable.

Good grief, he couldn't be expecting a *real* marriage, could he? Real as in sex and children? Ana had never actually discussed much relating to the marriage with Tati because in recent years Ana had spent most of her time in the family apartment in London. And when her cousin had come home to the country she'd often brought friends with her and Tati had not liked to intrude. Ana had once remarked that Tati couldn't clean and cook and then expect to socialise with her cousin's guests because that would be too awkward. Tati breathed in deep and slow to counter the pain of rejection that that recollection reawakened. Well, she guessed it would be quite a while before she had to cook and clean for her relatives again…if ever. And all of a sudden, her biggest apprehension assailed her, and she put out a hand and yanked at the Prince's sleeve to grab his attention.

'I have to be able to fly home regularly to visit my mother,' she told him apprehensively. 'Will that be allowed?'

I may be buying you, but I don't want to own you or be stuck with you round the clock, Saif almost replied before he thought better of being that frank.

'Of course,' he confirmed flatly, his attention on his seated father, who had regained his colour and his temper now that everyone was doing what *he* wanted them to do. Just as quickly Saif despised himself for even having that ungenerous thought.

Yet never had Saif more resented the reality that his father's state of health controlled him and deprived him of the options he should have had. His fierce love for his ailing parent warred against that resentment. Had he not had the fear of the Emir succumbing to a second heart attack after his first small attack some months earlier, Saif believed that he would have refused to marry a stranger. As it was, he dared not object. And what the hell was a sophisticated English socialite likely to find to do with herself in Alharia?

Why had his father selected such an unsuitable wife for him? Saif lifted his chin in wonderment at that question while the marriage celebrant droned on.

He would organise tutors for his bride, Saif decided, ensure that she studied their language, culture and history. If she wanted to be his wife so badly, if she was *this* determined to be rich and titled, then she would have to learn to fit in and not expect others to accommodate her. If he were to be cursed with a wife he could neither like nor respect, he would not allow her to also be an embarrassment to him.

'Sign your name,' he urged as he scrawled his own name on the marriage contract and handed his bride the pen.

Her palm perspiring, Tati scrawled her signature in the indicated spot. 'Is that it? I mean, when will the ceremony take place?'

'It's done,' Saif told her grimly. 'Excuse me.'

That was it? That was them *married*? Without even touching or indeed speaking? Tati was shaken and taken aback by his immediate departure.

'Are you happy now that it is done?' the Prince asked his father.

'Very,' the Emir confirmed with a nod of approval. 'And I hope that soon you will be happy as well.'

'May I ask why you wanted this for me?'

His elderly father regarded him with a frown. 'So that you will not be alone, my son. I am unwell. When I am gone, who will you have? I could not stand to think of you being alone.'

Saif swallowed the sudden unexpected thickness

clogging his throat, stunned by that simple explanation and the strong affection it conveyed, acknowledging that he had misjudged his father's intentions.
'But why…an Englishwoman?'

'I had no good fortune with the wives I married
and yet they were all supposedly wonderful local
matches. Like to like didn't work for me and I sought
a different experience for you. It is my hope that
your lively and sociable bride will make you relax.
You are a very serious young man and I thought she
might help you have some fun.'

'Fun,' Saif almost whispered, barely crediting that
such a word could have fallen from his strait-laced
father's lips.

'And provide you with company. Like you and
unlike me she is westernised and sophisticated and
you should have more in common.'

Saif was now ready to groan out loud. His father
believed that he was westernised and sophisticated
because he had spent five years abroad studying
business and working while the Emir had only spent
a matter of months out of Alharia and had never gone
travelling again. Saif, however, had spent more time
working to gain the necessary experience than in
clubs or bars.

Tati went through the hours that followed in a daze.
Men and women were segregated in the celebrations,
but Daliya was very keen to assure her that that was

the habit only in the Emir's household and that no such segregation was practised by the Prince or anyone else in Alharia. 'The Emir is as old as my great-grandfather,' Daliya told her in a polite excuse for what she clearly saw as an embarrassing practice.

In the all-women gathering where she was very much the centre of attention, Tati watched her aunt, Elizabeth Hamilton, partake of drinks and snacks and ignore her niece. Tati's rarely stirred temper began to spark at that point. She had learned the hard way to be hugely tolerant of other people's rude behaviour, but being studiously ignored by her aunt when her marrying Prince Saif had won her relatives a large amount of money left a bitter taste in her mouth.

She thought of all the humble pie she had eaten at Elizabeth's hands over the years and simmered in silence, too accustomed to restraint to surrender to the anger building inside her, the resentment that, *once again*, she was the fall guy even though she had not enjoyed even one day of the expensive lifestyle her aunt, uncle and cousin took for granted with their designer clothes and glamorous social lives. She and her mother had always scraped along, living cheap, never living well and never ever enjoying the choices and outings that the better off took for granted.

'It's time for you to leave,' Daliya whispered quietly. 'You have scarcely eaten, Your Highness.'

Your Highness, Tati thought in disbelief as she was escorted from the room and down all the endless corridors and up the staircases and across the halls to a totally different giant bedroom, where the maid who had unpacked her luggage in the room she was sharing with Ana already awaited her. Daliya and the maid together assisted her in removing the tunics and petticoats until at last she was down to the final layer, the sort of lingerie layer, she called it, and she finally felt as though she could breathe freely again.

'Where am I going now?' she enquired of Daliya.

'To Paris,' the brunette informed her with a beaming, envious smile. 'On your honeymoon trip.'

Oh, joy, Tati reflected, the angry resentment stirring afresh as she rustled through her slender wardrobe to extract clothing of her own in which to travel and tugged out a pair of leggings and a loose top, neither of which, she could see, satisfied Daliya, who, after asking permission with an anxious look, resorted to fumbling through Tati's case herself in search of something fancier.

'I don't have many clothes,' Tati muttered, mortified for the first time ever by that admission. Of course, she had a dress she had packed in case she got the chance to go to the wedding reception, she recalled wryly, but that slinky, glittery gown, which had originally belonged to Ana, wouldn't be remotely suitable for travelling.

'It is fine, Your Highness. It is more sensible to

travel in comfortable garments,' Daliya assured her
kindly.

Just as Tati was about to change, a knock sounded
briefly on the door and it opened without further
ado, framing Prince Saif—all flashing green eyes
and what Tati inwardly labelled 'temperament and
volatile with it'—who stalked into the room. He
instantly dominated his surroundings and her pair of
companions muttered breathless apologies for their
presence and immediately took themselves off.

My husband, Tati conceded in shock. *The stranger
I have married...*

'Now here we are at last with no more barriers
between us,' Prince Saif pointed out curtly.

All his bride wore was a silk shift. She *had* a
waist, a tiny one, and curves, distinctly sexy curves,
Saif noted unwillingly, for he was determined to see
no saving grace in the wife who had been forced on
him, although he could not help admiring that long
wheaten-blond hair that rippled down her spine like
a sheet of rumpled satin. Nor could a thin silk slip
hide the firm thrust of pouting breasts and prominent
nipples or the luscious shape of her highly feminine
bottom. Involuntarily Saif hardened and he clenched
his teeth against the throb of arousal, a natural response for a man whose sex life was, by virtue of
necessity, non-existent in Alharia. Only when Saif
travelled could he indulge his sensual appetites and

that amount of restraint did not come naturally to a young, healthy man, he allowed wryly.

Any reasonably attractive woman would turn him on at present, he assured himself, but, at the same time, Tatiana *was* his wife and that made quite a difference, he registered, wondering why that aspect had not occurred to him from the first. Yes, he could definitely do with a wife in that department. And what was more, the substitute was infinitely more to his taste than the original bride put forward. Unlike her cousin, Tati wasn't artificially enhanced to pout like a pufferfish on social media. Her lips had a naturally full pink pucker. She had a handful of freckles scattered across the bridge of her undeniably snub nose, but her face was still remarkably pretty, shaped like a heart with big blue eyes the colour of pansies.

Tati gazed back at him, heart starting to hammer inside her chest, breathing suddenly a challenge. 'Why are you staring at me?' she asked tightly.

'Why do you think? How many gold diggers do you think I meet and marry in the space of the same day?' Saif enquired with a lethal chill in his dark drawl, his shrewd green eyes glittering with sheer antipathy. 'And I am disgusted to find myself married to a woman willing to sell herself for money!'

Utterly unprepared for that attack coming out of nowhere at her, Tati whirled away from him, stabbed to the heart by his scorn. Of course, she hadn't thought beyond meeting her uncle's demands to ensure her mother's needs were met. Ridiculous as it was, she had rushed in where angels feared in too much of a hurry to consider what she was actually doing in marrying Prince Saif of Alharia for the wealth that would protect Mariana Hamilton's continuing care. But even as her shoulders drooped, they as quickly shot up again, roused by the fiercest anger she had ever felt.

'How dare you try to stand in judgement over me?' Tati launched back at him angrily. 'I did not sell myself for money and I am *not* a gold digger.'

Grudgingly amused by the way she straightened herself and stretched, as if she could magically gain a few inches of more imposing height just by trying, Saif regarded her coldly. 'From where I'm standing—'

'Yes, standing with your mighty dose of sexist prejudice on show!' Tati condemned wrathfully. 'You don't know what you're talking about because you don't know anything about me.'

'As you know nothing about me. You married me for cold, hard cash...or was it the title?'

'Why the heck would I *want* to be a princess? I wasn't one of those little girls who dressed up as one as a kid! And for that matter, if you're so darned fastidious and critical, why did you agree to marry a total stranger?'

'That is my private business,' Saif parried with a regal reserve that was infuriatingly intimidating.

A furious flush lit Tati's cheeks at that refusal to explain his motivation. 'Well, then, my reasons are my private business too!' she snapped back at him. 'I don't have to explain myself to you and I'm not going to even try. I'm quite happy for you to think of me as a gold digger, but I'm not selling myself or my body for cash! Be assured that there will be two blue moons in the sky and pigs flying before I get into a bed with you!'

Saif was outraged. He had never been exposed to such insolence before and her attitude came as a shock. Somehow, he had expected her to be ashamed when he confronted her, *not* defiant. 'If the marriage is not consummated, it is not a marriage and will be annulled,' he pointed out for no good reason other than the pride that would not allow her to believe that when it came to sex she could have any form of control over him.

'Is that some kind of a threat?' Tati yelled at him, barely recognising herself in the grip of the anger roaring through her slight body. She had simply been pushed around too much for one day. She was fed up with being forced to do what she didn't want to do, first by Ana refusing to face her own parents and then being bullied and threatened by her uncle. Now it seemed that the Prince, her husband, was trying to do the same thing. And she wasn't having it! In fact, she was absolutely done with people ordering her around and never saying thank you, taking her loyalty and gratitude for granted, acting as though they were the better person while they blackmailed and intimidated her!

Saif stilled, a very tall dark man who towered over her like a building. 'It is not. I do not threaten women. I simply voiced facts.'

'Right… OK.' Tati hovered, fighting to compose herself again when she had the most extraordinary desire to cry and shout and yell like an hysterical woman at the end of her tether. And that wasn't her, had never been her, she reminded herself. She had always been the calm, practical one compared to Ana, who flung a tantrum when she didn't get her own way and sulked for days. But for Tati, it had been a truly horrible long strain of a day and it was not done yet, and she did not feel that just then she had the necessary resources to cope with Saif's antagonism on top of everything else.

'I hate you,' she told him truthfully, because no guy that good-looking, who had *chosen* to marry her, had the right to tell her that she disgusted him. He was gorgeous to look at, but he had no manners, no decency and no sense of justice. If she were to blame for marrying him, he was equally to blame for marrying her. 'You're just one more person trying to blame *me* for *your* bad decisions!'

CHAPTER THREE

THE BRIDE AND the groom dined at opposite ends of the cabin.

A private jet, Tati acknowledged, covertly admiring the pale sleek leather and gleaming wood fitments in the cabin while telling herself firmly that she was not impressed. There were a lot of stewards on board as well. The level of contemporary luxury on the jet was not even remotely akin to the Victorian grandeur of the palace. A bundle of glossy fashion magazines was brought to her. She was waited on hand and foot and the meal that duly arrived was amazing. Only then did she appreciate that she was starving because she had barely eaten all day.

That terrible looming apprehension that had killed her appetite had drifted away, but the anger still lingered. Her face burned afresh at the recollection of being labelled a shameless gold digger. But wasn't that kind of woman what Prince Saif of Alharia deserved in a wife? After all, he had agreed to marry without demonstrating the smallest personal interest in his bride. He had not bothered to engineer a meeting or even a phone call with her cousin before the wedding! So, if he was displeased with the calibre of wife he had acquired, it was all his own fault! Still fizzing with resentment, Tati shot a glance down to the far end of the cabin where her husband was working on a laptop, once again showing off his indifference to the woman he had married. She wasn't one bit sorry that she had told him she hated him!

But my goodness, he was, as her mother would have said, 'easy on the eye.' Black hair tumbled across his brow, framing his hard, masculine profile. Those ridiculously long ebony lashes were a visible slash of darkness even at a distance and the curve of his shapely mouth was as obvious as the dark stubble beginning to shadow his jawline. Annoyingly, he kept on snatching at her attention. And she didn't know why he interfered with her concentration. Well, that was a lie, she acknowledged ruefully. A guy that gorgeous was kind of hard to ignore, especially if you had just married him, even though there was absolutely no way it would ever be a *real* marriage.

By the time the jet landed, Tati was smothering yawns. She was too incredibly weary to do more than disembark from the plane and climb into the limousine awaiting them without comment. The Prince was silent as well, probably busy brooding over the sheer indignity of being married off to a money-grubbing foreigner, she thought nastily. She had assumed they would be staying in a hotel, so it was a surprise when the limousine purred to a halt outside what appeared to be a rather large three-storey house in an affluent tree-lined street.

A little man in a smart jacket ushered them into a big opulent hall with a chandelier hanging overhead that was so spectacular she suspected it was antique Venetian glass. And she only knew that because her aunt Elizabeth had once had one made to look as though it were an antique and had regularly passed it off as such to impress her guests. Saif addressed the man in fluent French.

'Would you like a meal? A snack?' he then enquired politely of her.

'No, thanks. I just want to sleep for about a week.' Her face flamed as she belatedly realised that it was their wedding night and she stiffened, averting her attention from him in haste, although she didn't think he had any expectations whatsoever in that field. The look the Prince had given her when she had earlier told him she wasn't going to have sex with him should have frozen her to death where she stood. He had been outraged, but at least he hadn't argued. There was a bright side to everything, wasn't there?

'We will have to share a bed tonight,' Saif informed her in an undertone. 'We were expected to remain in Alharia until tomorrow. This place will not be fully staffed until then and only one bedroom has been prepared. Marcel is already apologising in advance for any deficiencies we may notice.'

The concept of having to share a bed with the Prince almost made Tati groan out loud. But she was too tired to fight with him. She didn't think he would make any kind of move on her. She was quite sure that she could have located linen and made up a bed for herself, but she was in a strange house, wary of treading on domestic toes and too drained to make a fuss. 'I'm too exhausted to care.'

It went without saying that she was not accustomed to such luxurious accommodation. Her aunt and uncle's home, Fosters Manor, was a pretty Edwardian country house but, as such houses went, it was not that large and it was definitely shabby. When her grandmother had still been alive, it had been beautifully kept, but maintenance standards had slipped once her uncle took over and dismissed most of the staff.

'It has been a long day,' Saif gritted, relieved she hadn't thrown a tantrum over the bed situation. He wasn't in the mood to deal with that.

Yet after the way he had confronted her with his opinion of her, it was little wonder that she had lost her temper with him, he conceded grudgingly. He had been insanely tactless when he had told her the truth of what he thought of her. It would have been more logical to swallow his ire because he was trapped in their marriage until such time as he was able to divorce her. On the other hand, he *could* take the annulment route, he reasoned thoughtfully. But that would upset his father, who would feel responsible for the whole mess because he had insisted that the wedding go ahead with the substitute bride.

He wondered if the little blonde beside him and the cousin who had taken flight had planned exactly this denouement. Clearly, her uncle had suspected her of that duplicity. Who would know her nature better than her own flesh and blood? Furthermore, anyone with the smallest knowledge of his father's character would have guessed that he would do virtually anything sooner than accept his son and heir being jilted. The Emir loathed scandal and he was very proud and touchy about any issue that might inflict a public loss of face on the throne. It seemed rather too neat that the original bride had vanished at the eleventh hour and her stand-in had appeared in her place, dressed as a traditional Alharian bride. He needed answers, Saif acknowledged, because now that she was his wife, he wanted to know precisely who and what he was dealing with. How calculating was she? How greedy? Could he make her less of a problem simply by throwing money at her? It was a distasteful idea but one he was willing to follow through on if it granted him peace.

Marcel cast open a door at the top of the stairs into a superb bedroom suite. Saif was reluctantly amused by the opulent appointments, thinking fondly that his half-brother, Angelino Diamandis, certainly knew how to live in luxury. Having worked hard to put any personal issues with his deserting mother behind him, he had gained sufficient distance from that betrayal to seek out his younger half-brother. A smile illuminated his lean dark features, softening his set jawline. If he was honest he occasionally envied his brother, Angel, for his freedom and independence, but he was not prepared to lose his father and step up to the throne to attain that same lack of constraint.

Barely able to credit how a single smile could light the Prince up to reveal ten times the charisma he had so far shown her, Tati got all flustered and heard herself ask, almost as if it were normal to speak to him civilly, 'Does this house belong to you?'

'No, it belongs to my—' Saif hesitated and swallowed what he had almost revealed, because he couldn't trust her with that information lest it reach the wrong ears. 'It belongs to a relative of mine. He offered it to me because he was unable to attend the wedding.' Well, at least *not* in his official capacity, Saif adjusted with a winning smile of satisfaction, for he had contrived to spend almost an hour with his brother that same afternoon. 'I prefer this to the anonymity of a hotel.'

'It's a fabulous place…from what little I've seen,' Tati adjusted awkwardly, moving past him to scoop up her toiletries bag and nightwear from the case that a maid had already begun to unpack, just as another had embarked on Saif's luggage. *Two* maids and yet supposedly the household was understaffed this evening?

As she bent down Saif stared, focused hungrily on her curvy bottom and the bounce of her full breasts as she straightened again, blond hair flaring like polished silk round her heart-shaped face, big blue eyes skittering off him at speed. She wouldn't meet his eyes. He didn't like that. It made him wonder what she was thinking, what she could be planning. The more he considered the manner in which she had immediately stepped into her cousin's shoes, the more suspicious he became of her every move. He winced at the current of lust still trying to pull him in a dangerous direction. Possibly an annulment would be the path to take if he could sell the idea to his father without shocking him too much. In the interim, he definitely needed to keep his hands off his bride.

Through an open door Tati could see a bathroom and she hastened into the sanctuary it offered. She didn't really need a bath but she ran one just the same, determined to make the most of her time alone. She took off the make-up, cleaned her teeth before finally lying back in hot, scented water and striving to relax. But how the heck could she relax with *him* out there? Ana would have charmed him out of the trees by now, she reflected ruefully. Men adored her cousin for her looks, her smiles and her flirtatious ways. Tati had never had that light, fluffy, girly vibe. She was sensible, practical, blunt. Life had made her that way, forcing her to be responsible. She loved her mother, but she had also learned very young that *she* had to look after her only parent, rather than the other way round.

Having a man in her life had been the least of her ambitions. Mariana had had a whole raft of unsuitable boyfriends, among them drunks, abusers and cheats. After Tati's first serious boyfriend, Dave, had ditched her to chase Ana instead, Tati had decided that men drummed up way too much drama in a woman's life. Once or twice, she had wished that she had got a little more experience out of the relationship and had tried out sex with Dave, because sometimes still being a virgin at her age made her feel out of step with the world she lived in. But the attraction had just never been strong enough for her to experiment with Dave and once he had succumbed to her cousin's allure, she had been relieved that she had held back.

An hour later, Tati emerged, flushed and soaked clean from the bathroom. Saif, casually clad in jeans and a black shirt, twisted round from his laptop to glance at her. His bride wore nothing suggestive, nothing even slightly sexy, so evidently seduction did not feature in her current plan. Saif strove to feel suitably relieved by that reassuring reality while wondering how the hell pink and white shorts with little bunnies on them and a plain white vest top could offer such dynamite appeal. It was all about shape, he reasoned abstractedly, a mathematical arrangement of feminine proportions in the exact combination that most appealed to the average male.

Evidently he was very much an average male, he decided, attention lingering on the smooth upper slopes of the soft firm breasts showing above the top, the shadow of the valley between, her tiny waist and the pleasing swell of the pert derriere that the clingy shorts enhanced. A pulse kicked up in his groin and he swung back to his work with a curse brimming on his lips.

'What are you working at?' she asked to break the taut silence, her face still flaming from his lengthy appraisal.

'I'm checking figures. I manage Alharia's investments,' Saif murmured tautly.

What had that long look of his been about, for goodness' sake? Tati supposed that she should have worn a dressing gown, but she hadn't packed one. Her inclusion in the trip to Alharia had been very much a last-minute thing, an added expense loudly objected to by Ana's parents. Ana, however, had said she could not go through with the wedding without Tati's support and that had got Tati on the flight, her case packed in a rush and not even full. She had left behind several items which she should have brought.

'Is the bathroom free now?' Saif enquired without turning round again.

Momentarily, Tati froze, mortified by her thoughtlessness: she was a bathroom hog. 'I'm sorry, I should've thought that you might want—'

'There must be a dozen such facilities in this property. Had I needed to do so, I could easily have found another.'

In silence, Tati nodded. 'Goodnight,' she said in a muffled tone and dived below the duvet.

Strange little creature, Saif decided, glancing at the bed, seeing her curled up in one small corner, only a tousled mop of blond hair showing above the duvet. If he hadn't known what he did know about her he might've thought that she was shy. He smothered a laugh at that ridiculous idea, shut down the accounts he had been working on and started to undress.

Tati peered out from under her hair and watched the jeans hit the polished floor in a heap. So, he was untidy as well as obnoxious, she thought without surprise, as he left them lying there and the shirt drifted down to join the jeans. He stretched in a fluid movement and for an instant she saw him standing there, naked but for a pair of boxers, every muscle flexing and pulling taut…and he had an awful lot of muscles enhanced by coffee-coloured skin that resembled oiled silk. Tati stared, remembering the ghastly charity calendar of half-naked men her mother had once put up on the wall. Mariana had accused her daughter of being a prude when Tati had said it embarrassed her.

But it *had* been an embarrassment to have that hanging in the kitchen, particularly after Ana had seen it and had told everybody at school. Tati had had to live through a barrage of sniggering 'dirty girl' abuse for weeks afterwards. Compared with Ana and her mother, she *was* a prude because, from what she had seen of their experiences, a more adventurous approach to men and sex more often led to hurt and disappointment than happiness.

Now watching Saif stretch and muscles ripple across his hard, corrugated abdomen and down the length of his smooth brown back, Tati reminded herself that it was just a body, truly a more blessed body than most men rejoiced in but simply a body, an arrangement of bones, flesh and muscle that every single living person had. Only that very grounded outlook did not explain why she was still staring and why she had a hot, tight, clenched sensation tugging at the junction of her thighs. She had stared because he was beautiful, and she hadn't realised that a man could be beautiful that way. *Really, Tati*, she mocked her excuse. All that Adam and Eve stuff in the Bible hadn't tipped her off about that essential attraction? Cheeks hot enough to fry eggs on, she rolled over and buried her face in the cool pillows, trying not to listen to the distant sound of water running in the shower.

Saif was unaccustomed to sharing a bed and his bride's every movement disturbed him, reminded him of her existence and pushed rudely past his wall of reserve. He couldn't ignore her, he couldn't forget the allure of those eyes with the velvety appeal of a flower, her pale slender thighs or her surprisingly full breasts. That failure to maintain his usual mental discipline only made him even angrier with her. As he lay awake, he came up with a plan as to how to keep her occupied and marvelled at its simplicity. He could send her out day after day...

Tati wakened in the early hours because she felt cold. As she flipped over, she discovered the reason: the duvet had been stolen. That fast, she remembered that she was sharing a bed and she dug two hands into the bedding and yanked her side of it back with violent determination. Saif sat up with a jerk and flashed on the light.

'I was cold,' Tati announced in a snappish tone of defence and she hunched under the section of duvet she had reclaimed, turning her back on him.

Saif thought with satisfaction of the bride-free day ahead of him and lay back down. Even hunched in the bedding, she contrived to look unbearably alluring. How could she make him want her so much? Were a few sexless weeks sufficient to make him desperate? He lay there thinking of the many sensual ways he could have raised his bride's temperature without recourse to warmer bedding. Just considering those pursuits, indeed leafing through them with the intensity of an innate sensualist, left Saif as hard as a rock and it was dawn when he finally gave up trying to rest and rose to start work again.

The maid bringing her breakfast wakened Tati. She sat up while the curtains were being opened and registered that she was alone in the bed and expected to eat there. Pushing her hair off her brow, she accepted the tray, setting it down again once the maid had gone and scrambling into the bathroom to freshen up before she ate.

While she was enjoying her cup of tea and a buttery, flaky, delicious croissant, the Prince strode in. Saif emanated pure sophistication and sleek good looks in his perfectly tailored dark business suit. Involuntarily, her mouth ran dry, her tummy fluttering, responses she struggled to suppress. Expensive fabric outlined and enhanced his wide shoulders, his narrow hips and long, strong legs. He was very well built…as she had cause to know after ogling him while he undressed the night before, she reminded herself irritably. He was also infuriatingly calm and in control while she still felt as though her life had lurched off track without warning and fallen into a very large, very deep pothole.

As she sat there, Tati was extremely tense, her

fingers locked tight to her china cup. It had occurred to her for the first time that she had overlooked one very obvious point of dissension between them. Saif had expected to marry her glamorous, sexy cousin and had instead ended up with her dull, plain and unsexy substitute. Of course, he was disappointed; of course, he was angry. No man would choose Tati in place of Ana, she reflected painfully. 'I'll sort out another bedroom for me to use tonight,' she proffered stiffly, meaning it as an olive branch of sorts in the aftermath of the duvet tussle.

In the sunlight slanting through the windows, the brilliant green eyes locked to her were as jewelled and intense as polished emeralds. All of a sudden, a bizarre level of annoyance was gripping Saif. Evidently it was one thing for him to want to be rid of her, but another thing entirely when she appeared to return the compliment. 'That will not be necessary,' he began before he could question the far from sensible reaction steering him off course.

Tati tilted her chin. 'It's necessary,' she pointed out. 'I don't think either of us could have got much sleep last night.'

Saif discovered that he did not like being told what was necessary by *her*. It set his even white teeth on edge and brought out a self-destructive edge of pique he had not known until that instant that he possessed. 'We will *continue* to share the same room.'

'But why on earth would we?' Tati exclaimed with incredulity.

'You wanted this marriage… *Live with it!*' Saif spelt out without apology or, indeed, further explanation. Even had he tried to do so, he could not have explained the gut instinct that was driving him because he did not know what had roused it or even what it meant.

'You know…' Tati began, her chest heaving with a sudden dragged-in breath, furious that he appeared to be taking out his disappointment that Ana wasn't his bride on her…as though it were *her* fault. Did he think that? And shouldn't she know by now what he was thinking? The lack of communication between them was only adding to their problems. 'Sometimes, you make me want to hit you!'

'I noticed the streak of violence in your family when your aunt attempted to slap you. Make no attempt to assault me. There is no reason in the world why we should descend to such a degrading level,' the Prince asserted.

His mind was wandering again, questioning how she could utter such a threat while still looking so fresh and tempting. It was first thing in the morning as well and her hair was tousled and she had utilised not a scrap of cosmetic enhancement that he could see. Indeed, in harsh daylight her porcelain skin had an amazingly luminous quality that confounded his every expectation. She might be a substitute; she might be everything he despised in the wife he had not wanted in the first place, but one truth was inescapable: she was much more of a beauty than he had initially been prepared to acknowledge.

'You don't even have a sense of humour, do you?' Tati gasped, staring accusingly at him.

'I have made arrangements for your entertainment today,' Saif informed her smoothly, refusing to react in any way to the charge of a lack of humour. Certainly, he found nothing about their current situation worthy of amusement.

'How very kind of you,' Tati muttered tautly, wondering what was coming next.

'I have hired a team of personal shoppers to give you a tour of the best retail outlets in Paris,' the Prince completed.

Send the little woman out shopping, Tati thought furiously. He simply wanted her out of his hair. And what did you do with a gold digger when you wanted peace? Throw money at her! And when you had more money than a gold mine, throwing money was the easy option. Tati clamped her teeth together hard on a sarcastic response. She recalled her Granny Milly telling her that you caught more flies with honey than vinegar. But sheer rage rippled through her in a heady wave that left her almost light-headed because she wasn't some greedy tramp the Prince could tempt, control and ultimately debase with cold, hard cash!

'How wonderful,' Tati told him with a serene

smile. 'I shall feel as though all my Christmases have come at once. Do I have a budget?'

Saif interpreted the glitter in her big blue eyes as pure avarice. 'No budget,' he retorted with a flashing smile of reassurance.

He was giving her a free ticket to spend, spend, spend and she would be sure not to disappoint him. After all, if ever a guy deserved to have his worst expectations met, it was Saif, and she would *enjoy* playing the gold-digging bride, she told herself fiercely. If anything, he would learn to know better than to send her out shopping in one of the most expensive cities in the world without a budget.

She put on her jeans. Her brain could still not quite encompass the reality that the Prince was now *her* husband instead of her cousin's. He didn't even act as a husband would, did he? Well, like a very reluctant one, she decided ruefully. Possibly he hadn't wanted to get married either.

My goodness, maybe that could even explain why he had been married off in the first place…was it possible that the Prince was gay? And that he had been married off to conceal the fact? But if that were true, why, given the opportunity, wouldn't he have wanted to claim a bedroom of his own?

Tati frowned and conceded that Saif was a mass of confusing contradictions. He insisted they *had* to share a bedroom. For the sake of appearances? Did he want their marriage to look normal even if it wasn't? Out of pride or out of necessity? If he was gay and if it was impossible for his father to accept him as such, their crazy marriage made sense. Of course, understanding didn't make her like Saif any better for the way he had accused her of being a gold digger.

In fact, she hated him for that. Tati had spent her entire life being pushed around and put down by those who had more power than she had. Her own relatives had done that to her and, even before her mother had succumbed to dementia, Mariana had urged her daughter not to 'rock the boat' by defending her. Sadly, swallowing her pride and turning the other cheek had never improved matters in the slightest for Tati. In fact, that attitude, both at school and at home, had only made the bullying worse. And she wasn't prepared to settle for that again, for being abused when she hadn't done anything wrong, for being insulted simply because she was poor and had fewer options than other people. Her head came up, her chin lifting. No. No way was His Royal Highness the Crown Prince of Alharia about to get away with doing her down as well!

Thirty minutes later, Tati stepped into a long cream limousine containing three very ornamental and chatty women. At first glance, she could see that she was a surprise, a disappointment, in that she wasn't as decorative as they had expected and, as it was normal for her to want to please people and she fully intended to spend, spend, spend as directed by her bridegroom, she said, 'I need a whole new wardrobe!'

And the smiles broke out, betraying the visible relief that she was likely to be a keen buyer. Presumably, her companions worked on commission and why shouldn't they profit from her pressing need for clothes? Starting with nightwear and lingerie, she required everything. It was one thing to be proud and independent, another thing entirely to be the most poorly or inappropriately dressed person in the room. And she had no plans to start washing and drying her knickers in the nearest bathroom any time soon. In fact, she had to suppress a giggle as she attempted to picture the Prince's reaction. She doubted that he had ever been exposed to that kind of common touch.

The first stop on their trip was the Avenue Montaigne, a tree-lined thoroughfare packed with high-end fashion outlets. Aside from the uneasy acknowledgement that her cousin, Ana, would have truly revelled in such an opportunity, Tati concentrated on the practicalities of buying as much as she possibly could without ever consulting a price tag lest it send her into shock. She strayed from one designer boutique to the next with her companions, having by then established her preferences, working hard to locate the casual and formal items she specified. They moved on to the Boulevard Saint Germain, where she found chic dresses aplenty and the shoes and bags to team with them. She eventually succumbed to the temptation of putting on a new outfit. They visited a trendy rooftop café, where she enjoyed the spectacular views of the city and drank champagne. Of lunch there was no sign and only a handful of nuts came her way.

Mid-afternoon, she was professionally made up and equipped with enough cosmetics to provide a makeover for half a city block. Perfume specially mixed for her came next and she loved the perfume as much as the professional jargon of the scent world, which talked of hints of jasmine and spice, redolent of hotter climes. She allowed herself to be talked into buying a new phone and a new watch as well.

The guilt of enjoying herself while being wildly extravagant soon engulfed her in a tide. She had spent, spent, *spent* to hit back at Saif for his condemnation of her when in truth he knew nothing about her and evidently didn't care to find out anything about her either. But only on the drive back to the house, while her companions were cheerfully breaking out the champagne again to celebrate a successful day of shopping, did she ask herself how meeting every one of Saif's worst expectations of her character could benefit her in any way. She refused the champagne because she wasn't in the mood to rejoice.

What had she done? Why had she let her raging resentment at her position and his attitude take over and drive her? Why had she set out to prove that she was every bit as greedy as he had assumed she was?

A severe attack of the guilts gripped Tati as she watched a procession of staff march through the echoing hall to deliver the boxes and bags of her accumulated shopping upstairs to the bedroom. There they would proceed to unpack and organise her many, many purchases before storing them in the empty drawers and closets. She flopped down on an opulent couch in the drawing room, her face burning with mortification as she pictured the sweater she had bought in *four* different colours. The cringe factor was huge because in all her life she had never made an extravagant purchase before.

When would she contrive to wear a sweater in a desert kingdom? Presumably, she would wear the winter garments when she went home to visit her mother, she reasoned weakly. As for the fancy dresses, the high heels and all the elegant separates, where was she planning to wear them? Observation currently suggested that the Prince she had married would be in no hurry to take her anywhere, particularly now that she had shown what he would no doubt deem to be her true colours. And yet she had *needed* clothes, she thought wretchedly, for not only had she packed very little to fly out to Alharia for what she had assumed would be a very short stay, but she also had nothing much worthy of packing back home. The kind of casual wear she had worn to run her aunt and uncle's household wouldn't pass muster in her current role.

But neither of those facts excused her extravagance. She could have gone to a chain store to cover her requirements and only bought the necessities, she conceded unhappily. Instead she had shopped and spent recklessly in some of the most exclusive designer shops in the world.

Marcel brought her tea and tiny dainty macarons on a silver tray. She glanced up when she heard a step in the hall and saw Saif still in the doorway. He had shed his jacket and tie and his sculpted jawline was shadowed with stubble. His gorgeous green eyes clashed with hers and she felt hot all over as if she had been exposed to a flame. She went pink and shifted uneasily on her seat, her mouth running very dry.

Saif was trying very hard not to gape at the blonde beauty on the opulent sofa. Like a fine jewel once displayed in an unworthy setting, she had been reset and polished up to perfection since their last meeting. A dark off-the-shoulder top clung to her like a second skin, lovingly hugging pert full breasts and skin that looked incredibly perfect and smooth. A short skirt in some kind of toning print exposed slender knees and shapely calves leading down to small feet shod in strappy heels. Off the scale arousal inflamed Saif as fast as a shot of adrenalin in his veins. An uncomfortable throb set up an ache at his groin.

Tati gazed back at him, dismay and a leaping hormonal response that unnerved her darting through her tense body. She found it utterly impossible to look away from Saif. His raw desirability was that intense from his tousled black hair to the rich green deep-set eyes fringed with ebony lashes that magnetised her.

'We have to talk,' she told him awkwardly. 'We have to sort stuff out.'

His half-brother, Angelino, the consummate playboy, had once told Saif that the minute a woman mentioned the need to talk, a sensible man should go straight into avoidance mode. Saif collided warily with huge blue-pansy-coloured eyes and parted his lips to shut her down.

'Please,' Tati added in near desperation. 'Because right now, everything's going crazy and wrong.'

'Is it?'

He did not know why he questioned that statement when he should have agreed because the arousal afflicting him was both crazy and wrong. He *had* to remain detached and in control. Nothing good could come from giving in to his baser instincts; nothing good could come from him backing down when confronted with her feminine wiles. And those flowery eyes of hers were shimmering with what might have been tears, her full lower lip quivering. The sight stabbed him to the heart, and he strode forward, a forceful, instantaneous urge to fix whatever was wrong powering him.

'Tatiana,' he began, determined to continue the conversation in private where they could be neither overheard nor seen. It was second nature for Saif to consider appearances, raised as he had been in a palace swarming with staff where keeping secrets was an almost impossible challenge.

'Nobody calls me that,' she told him in a wobbly voice.

'Except me. I will not call you Tatty like your relatives. It is an insult and I don't know why you've allowed it.' Without another word, Saif bent down and scooped her off the couch as if she were no heavier than a doll.

'What are you doing?' she exclaimed in stark disconcertion.

'Taking you upstairs where we may be assured of discretion,' the Prince countered, striding out across the hall with complete cool as if carrying a woman around were an everyday occurrence for him.

'Why on earth would we need discretion?' Tati queried nervously. 'You can put me down now.'

'You were becoming distressed… *Crying!*' Saif pointed out with a raw edge to his dark, deep drawl.

'I wasn't crying!' Tati protested, highly offended by the charge. 'I don't cry. You could torture me and I wouldn't cry! Just sometimes my eyes flood when I'm upset—it's a nervous thing but I don't start crying, for goodness' sake! I'm not a little girl!'

'No, definitely *not* a little girl except in height,' Saif quipped, pushing through the bedroom door to set her down on the big bed. 'Now tell me, why are you upset?'

'Because I let you *goad* me into behaving badly today and I'm furious with myself and with you!' Tati told him roundly. 'I went out today and spent a fortune on clothing because—'

'I urged you to…how is that bad behaviour?' Saif prompted, his gaze locked to the beautiful eyes angrily fixed to him, his fingers rising to brush back the silky blond hair rippling across her cheekbone. The long strands fell over his wrist, pale wheaten gold against his skin.

That light touch that seemed perilously close to a caress made Tati shiver while her skin broke out in goosebumps of awareness. 'You don't understand…'

'The only thing I understand right now is that I want you,' Saif breathed in the driven tone of harsh sincerity, his beautiful jewelled eyes smouldering as she looked up at him.

'Me? You want…*me*?' Tati almost whispered in disbelief and wonderment.

'Why wouldn't I want you?' Saif turned the question back on her in equal surprise. 'You are a remarkable beauty.'

That was a heady compliment for a woman who

had never been called beautiful in her entire life, who had always been in the shadows, either unnoticed or passed over or summarily dismissed as being unimportant. Tati stared at him in astonishment and she was so blasted grateful for that tribute that she stretched up and kissed his cheek in reward.

As her breasts momentarily pressed into his chest and the intoxicating scent of her engulfed him, the soft invitation of her lips on his skin burned through Saif's self-discipline like a fiery brand and destroyed it. Without any hesitation, he closed her slight body into the circle of his arms and brought his mouth crashing down on hers with a hunger he couldn't even attempt to control.

Oh, wow, Tati thought abstractedly, *wasn't expecting this, wasn't expecting to feel* this...

CHAPTER FOUR

AND THIS WAS the amazing sign that Tati had always been waiting and hoping to feel in a man's arms: electrified, exhilarated, physically aware of her own body to the nth degree. Only until that moment she had honestly believed that that kind of reaction was simply a myth, something that some women chose to exaggerate, which didn't truly exist. But with that single kiss Saif had knocked Tati right out of her complacent assumptions, knocked her sideways and upside down and just at that moment, regardless of whether it made sense or not, her stupid body was humming as fiercely as an engine getting revved up at the starting line.

'So…er…you're not gay,' Tati commented weakly as he released her mouth and dragged in a shuddering breath. 'Obviously.'

Saif gazed down at her in complete astonishment. 'Why would you think I was gay?'

'Your father marrying you off like that, not caring that I was a substitute for the bride that he had chosen,' Tati pointed out breathlessly. 'It seemed like he didn't care who you married as long as a marriage took place.'

'It *was* like that. All of Alharia knew that it was my wedding day. My father viewed the bride's disappearance as an absolute humiliation and an outrage against the throne itself. He could not accept that shame. As long as a wedding took place and he could cover up what really happened, he was appeased,' Saif explained, a lingering frown drawing his sleek dark brows together.

'I didn't appreciate how far-reaching the effects of Ana running away would be,' Tati admitted. 'I didn't understand that it would be such a crime and an embarrassment in your father's eyes either... I was stupidly naïve.'

'Kiss me again,' Saif husked, his attention locked to the full pink lower lip she was worrying at with the edge of her small blunt teeth.

'I'm not sure that we should.'

'Nothing that tastes as good as your mouth could be wrong,' Saif told her.

'Quite the poet when you want to be,' Tati whispered, barely breathing as she looked into those stunning green eyes of his and felt the flutter of butterflies in her tummy and the wicked heat of anticipation. A 'what the heck?' sensation that felt unfamiliar but somehow very, very right was assailing her. Other people took risks all the time, but she never did and the acknowledgement rankled.

'We are married.'

She wasn't thinking about that, all she was thinking about was how he made her *feel* and that felt wildly self-indulgent, something she never allowed herself to be. But what were a few kisses? No harm in that, no lasting damage, she reasoned with determination. Why did she always stress herself out by trying to second-guess stuff? Why did she take life so seriously and always behave as though the roof were likely to fall on her if she deviated from her set path of rectitude? In a resentful surge of denying that fretful and serious habit of generally looking on the downside of life, she tipped her head back and said tautly, 'So we are...'

Saif tasted her soft pink mouth, which had all the allure of a ripe peach, and then he yielded even more to the hunger storming through his tall, powerful frame, nudging her back against the pillows, a lean hand gliding up from a slender knee to skate along the stretch of her thigh.

Tati gasped, her hips rising, her thighs clenching on the sudden ache stabbing at the heart of her. It was terrifyingly intense. 'You make me want you... I don't know how!' she exclaimed helplessly, every nerve ending in her body on the alert.

Saif smiled down at her, green eyes aglow with

energy below well-defined brows. 'You know how…
you're not that innocent.'

But she was, she *was*, she conceded uneasily, because absolutely everything felt so novel and fresh
and exciting for her. And why wouldn't it when she
had never felt that way before? He shifted over her,
one long, strong leg sliding between hers, and her
breath snarled in her throat, her tummy fluttering
with an incandescent mix of nerves and craving that
left her light-headed. He kissed her again, parting
her lips, delving between, his tongue flicking across
the roof of her mouth, making delicious little quivers
circulate through her lower body.

The weight of him against her, the clean, musky,
all-male scent of him engulfing her, the way he
plucked at her lower lip and teased it with the edge
of his teeth. It all drove her a little crazy, igniting an
insane impatience that made her fingers spread and
dig into his shirt-clad back, needing to touch the skin
below the cotton, clawing it up to finally learn that
he was every bit as hot in temperature as his kisses
promised. She squirmed up into the sheltering heat
of him and he pressed his lips to the slender column
of her throat, discovering yet another place that was
extraordinarily sensitive, tracing it down to the valley between her breasts.

Saif pulled her top over her head and cast it aside.
His big hands spread to cup the full swell of her
breasts cupped in lace-edged silk. His thumbs found

her prominent nipples, stroked, and an arrow of heat speared down into her groin, making her hips rise. The bra melted away and she barely noticed because the feel of his hands on her naked skin sent literal shivers of response through her. He lowered his head over the pouting mounds and employed his mouth on the straining peaks, and she discovered a new sensual torment that utterly overwhelmed her as his tongue lashed the swollen buds and set up a chain reaction inside her that increased the ache tugging between her thighs.

He brushed away her last garment and her whole body rose as he finally touched her *there* where she had the most powerfully indecent craving to be touched. A light forefinger scored across the most sensitive spot of all and her spine arched, a gasp parting her lips. Her hand travelled up from his shoulder into his ruffled black hair and rifled through the silky strands to draw him back down to her again.

He nuzzled her parted lips, plucked at the full lower one with the edge of his teeth, teasing and rousing while he traced the damp, silky flesh between her thighs. She moaned and shifted her hips, the fiery pulse beating at her core rising in intensity in concert with her heartbeat. As he circled the most tender spot, the sizzling desire thrumming through her took an exponential leap and her fingers dug into his scalp as she fought for control. She wanted more, she *needed* more, she wanted him inside her to sate the tormenting hollow ache. She didn't recognise herself in the blind hold of that overwhelming craving.

Indeed she was at the agonising height of anticipation when Saif suddenly stopped dead and stared down at her with green eyes glittering with frustration. 'I don't have contraception here.'

'I'm on the pill…it doesn't matter!' Tati gasped.

'I have not been with anyone since a recent health check.'

Unaccustomed to such sensible conversations even while accepting that they were necessary, Tati could feel the heat of embarrassment burning her already flushed cheeks. 'I haven't been with anyone either,' she hastened to assure him.

Relief flooded his expressive gaze. 'I wasn't expecting this…*us*,' he admitted tautly, rearranging her under him, unzipping his trousers.

The instant she felt the satin-smooth touch of him against her entrance she tipped her legs back, hungry for the experience. He pushed into her slowly and she tensed at that strange sensation, closing her eyes tight and gritting her teeth momentarily when the sting and burn of his invasion broke through the barrier of her virginity. It hurt but not as much as she had feared it might. In fact, if there was such a thing, it was a *good* hurt, she reasoned abstractedly, her ability to concentrate still utterly controlled by that overriding hunger for the fulfilment that only he could give her.

Pleasure skated along her nerve endings as he bent her further back and drove deeper into her needy depths. Excitement climbed as he picked up his pace and her heart began to thump inside her, her breath catching in her throat. The whole of her being was caught up in the tightening bands of tension in her pelvis that merely pushed the craving higher and then the storm of gathering excitement coalesced in one bright, blinding instant. Like fireworks flaring inside her, it was electrifying. The excitement pushed her over the edge in an explosion of incredible pleasure that engulfed her in a sweet after-tide of blissful release. She tumbled back into the pillows, winded and drained but feeling light as a feather.

Saif achieved completion with a shuddering groan of relief and quickly pulled away from her, afraid of crushing her tiny body beneath his weight. He flung himself back and whispered, 'I've never had sex without a condom before. That was…unexpectedly…much more exciting than I ever dreamt…but you…you were *amazing*,' he stressed, locking brilliant green eyes to her burning face with sensual appreciation.

Tati's light-as-a-feather sensation was fast fading and the regrets were kicking in even faster. 'How did this happen?' she whispered shakily. 'We don't even like each other—'

'Speak for yourself. I like you very much indeed

at this moment,' Saif countered with dancing eyes of amusement.

Tati was remarkably disgruntled by that light-hearted comment. There he lay, confident, calm and absolutely in control, while she felt as if she were falling to pieces inside herself. She couldn't believe that she had had sex with him, didn't want to accept that she had urged him on like a shameless hussy. A strand of nagging anxiety pierced her.

'Did you…er…withdraw?' she mumbled in mortification, ashamed that she hadn't noticed, hadn't thought to suggest, hadn't acted on a single intelligent thought.

'Why would I have done that when you are protected by contraception?' Saif enquired.

Tati said nothing but she paled. She had left her contraceptive pills behind in the rush of packing for Alharia and could only wonder how effective those pills would be when she had already missed a couple of doses. She had never had to worry about anything like that before because she was only taking the pills in the first place to ease a difficult menstrual cycle.

Saif sat up. 'I need a shower… I'll use the one next door.' He sprang out of bed, stark naked and unself-conscious. 'We could share it…it's a big shower.'

'I don't think so,' she said flatly, downright incredulous at the suggestion that they could share a shower.

He didn't need to be self-conscious with his lean,

athletic physique, she thought ruefully, but, person-
ally speaking, she would not be getting out of bed
in front of him without sucking her tummy in to
the best of her ability. As she watched, he flipped
through drawers and brought out fresh clothing to
pull on trousers and a fresh shirt and stride out of
the room.

How on earth could she have been stupid enough
to have sex with him? How the heck had that happened? She hadn't been her usual self, she reasoned
ruefully—she had been angry, guilty and upset about
the situation she was in and ashamed of her extravagance. But then *somehow* curiosity and desire had
combined to blow all common sense out of the water,
she reflected unhappily as she darted out of bed and
raced into the dressing room to extract fresh under-
wear before speeding into the bathroom.

Where would she be if she fell pregnant? She had
just had unprotected sex and she knew the risks. Her
parents hadn't conceived her by choice. She had been
an accident, conceived at a party with a man with
whom her mother had had only a casual relationship.
In every way, never mind her birth father's eventual
arrest for fraud, Tati had been a mistake even if her
mother had made the best of her arrival and had always assured her daughter that she had no regrets
whatsoever.

As he stripped again next door, Saif was thinking
that he would buy his bride something special as a

mark of his appreciation. She deserved a handsome gift for not holding against him the cruel accusations he had made. He had been harsh and much less generous but that *had* to change, he acknowledged ruefully, because Tatiana was his wife and, for as long as they were together, she had a right to both his respect and his care. Just as he was about to switch the water on, he noticed the streak of blood on his thigh and he stopped dead with a frown.

When Tati emerged from the bathroom, she was fully dressed and unprepared to find that Saif was waiting for her. His impact stole the breath from her lungs. Black hair still damp from the shower, his lean dark features unnervingly grave, he was strikingly handsome. Tailored black trousers outlined his long powerful thighs and his plain white shirt was open at his throat. He was the very definition of casual, elegant sophistication.

'Is there something wrong?' she prompted, striving to appear more composed than she indeed felt.

'Before I showered, I noticed that there was blood on me... I must know—did I hurt you?'

Tati's face flamed crimson because she was utterly unprepared for that question. 'A little, but it's par for the course, isn't it...the first time, I mean?' she completed awkwardly, trying to pass it off casually, wishing he simply hadn't noticed anything amiss.

Saif froze in astonishment. 'You *were* a virgin?'

'Yes. Let's not make a fuss about it,' Tati urged tightly.

'It is not something I can ignore… I am guilty of having made assumptions about you, assumptions that clearly have no basis in fact,' Saif breathed tautly, far less comfortable after she had made that confirmation.

Tati breathed in deep and slow, but it still didn't suppress the rage hurtling up through her. 'So, because I was greedy, I also had to have been… What do we call it? Around the block a few times?' she paraphrased with a grimace.

'At twenty-four most young women have some sexual experience,' Saif countered, standing his ground on that score.

'But I'm not twenty-four. I'm twenty-one… Within a few weeks of my next birthday, but not quite there yet,' Tati filled in thinly, her spine rigid as she moved to the door. 'Perhaps you should find out a little more about me before you start judging.'

'I am not judging you,' Saif countered with measured cool.

'You've been judging me from the moment you met me, and it stops here and now,' Tati told him, lifting her chin in challenge, her accusing blue eyes bright as sapphires. 'Clearly you weren't any keener on this marriage than I was, but I'm done taking all the blame for it! I've been pushed around and used by my cousin and then by my uncle and aunt but I'm *not* going to accept being pushed around and used by you as well!'

With that ringing assurance, Tati stalked out of the room, her short skirt flipping round her slender knees, her breasts taut and firm and highly noticeable from the rigid angle of her spine. Challenged to drag his attention from her, Saif swore under his breath, rebelling at the temptation to follow her and argue. He didn't do arguments with women. He didn't do drama. He didn't believe that he had ever pushed around or *used* any woman. He had been force-fed his father's deep suspicions of the opposite sex from an early age and had done his utmost to combat that biased mindset with his intelligence.

Yet he had never wanted to fall in love and run the risk of giving up control of his emotions to a woman and trusting her. The rejection dealt by the mother who had deserted him had cut him deep down inside. He had learned to live with that reality, though, by burying his sensitivity on that issue.

And life experience had made him more cynical. He had been used by women, used for sex, for money, chased and feted by those in search of status and a title. Once or twice when he was younger and more naïve, he had been hurt. As a result, he was *not* prejudiced, he was *wary*, he reflected grimly.

CHAPTER FIVE

As TATI REACHED the foot of the sweeping staircase without any idea of where she was going, she was intercepted by Marcel and shown across the hall into a dining room with a table already beautifully set for a meal. She took a seat with alacrity because she was more than ready to eat. She had been hungry even before she got into bed with her prince, she thought wildly, although she had done nothing there worthy of the excuse of having worked up an appetite. That belated reflection birthed a host of insecurities. She had lain there like a statue, she thought in dismay, as much of a partner as a blow-up doll. The slow-burning heat of mortification crept up through her like a living flame and it was not eased by Saif's sudden entrance into the dining room.

'I forgot about dinner,' he said almost apologetically.

'I didn't get lunch either,' she hastened to admit.

'Why not?' Saif queried, his startlingly light eyes bright against his olive skin.

'Nobody else seemed to be interested in eating.' Tati shrugged, still fascinated by those eyes of his.

Saif frowned as Marcel arrived with little plates. 'It was for you to say that you wished to eat,' he told her gently. 'You were the client. You were in charge.'

Stiffening at that veiled criticism, Tati looked down at her plate and shook out her napkin. 'I usually go with the majority vote and endeavour to fit in.'

As Tati shifted awkwardly in her seat, in the silence the dulled ache at the heart of her almost made her wince, and recalling exactly how she had acquired that intimate ache made her flush to the roots of her hair. In haste she began to eat, struggling to suppress the overwhelming memory of his lean, powerful body sliding over and inside hers, the heart-thumping excitement that had gripped her and the sheer unvarnished pleasure of it.

As Marcel arrived with the main course, she glanced up, desperate to distract herself from such thoughts. 'Your green eyes... So unexpected, so unusual,' she heard herself remark gauchely, inwardly cringing from the surprise that lit up those extraordinary eyes of his.

'I inherited them from my mother,' Saif proffered, amused by her embarrassment and how little she was able to hide it from him. 'I don't know where she got them from or if anyone else in her family shares them because I have no contact with her family.'

'Why's that?' Tati pressed, unable to stifle her interest.

'You really don't know anything about me, do you?' Saif registered. 'My mother ran off with another man six months after my birth, deserting me and my father. Her family took offence when my father spoke his opinion too freely of her behaviour.'

'My goodness, that was tough for both of you. What was it like growing up, torn between two parents? I presume they divorced?'

'Yes, there was a divorce. I have no memory of her, though, and I was never torn between them. She never asked to see me. She wiped her first marriage out of her life as though it had never happened.'

Tati grimaced. 'That was very sad for you.'

'Not really,' Saif countered, his jawline stiffening as he made that claim. 'I had three very much older half-sisters, who devoted themselves to my care in her place.'

'How much older?'

'They were born of my father's first marriage and are in their sixties now. I was spoiled as the long-awaited son and heir,' Saif told her quietly. 'I have much to be grateful for.'

He had dealt with his troubled background with such calm and logic that she was slightly envious, conscious that she had more often been mortified by her own. She dealt him a wry glance. 'You notice that we're talking about everything but the elephant in the room.'

'I didn't want to give you indigestion by mentioning our marriage,' Saif delivered straight-faced.

Tati stared at him, entrapped by those striking eyes as green as emeralds in his lean dark face, and then her defences crumbled as she spluttered and then laughed out loud, grabbing up her water glass to drink and ease her throat. 'So, you *do* have a sense of humour.'

'Yesterday was trying for *both* of us,' he pointed out as he pushed away his plate and leant back fluidly in his chair to give her his full attention.

'Why did you agree to go ahead with the marriage?'

'My father has a serious heart condition. I didn't want to risk refusing to marry you and stressing his temper,' Saif admitted grimly. 'He needs to remain calm, which is often a struggle for him.'

Tati was disconcerted by that admission. It had not occurred to her that he might have an excuse as good as her own for letting the ceremony proceed. That knocked her right off the moral high ground she had been unconsciously hugging like a blanket while silently blaming him for being willing to marry her.

He hadn't had a choice either.

'You must've been disappointed that I wasn't my cousin, Ana,' she said uncomfortably.

'Why would I have been? She was a stranger too.'

'Yes, but she's much prettier than I am and she's sophisticated and lively. I'm none of those things. Ana's one of the beautiful people… I'm a nobody.'

'How a *nobody*?' Saif framed, his nostrils flaring with distaste. 'She is your cousin. I assume you have led similar lives.'

Tati breathed in fast and deep as Marcel arrived with a mouth-watering selection of desserts. 'Not for me, thank you,' she said in creditable French.

'Saif,' she said quietly once Marcel had departed. 'You married the poor relation, not the family princess. I'm illegitimate and my birth father, whom I never met, was imprisoned for fraud. He's dead now.'

'Why are you telling me this?' he demanded.

'You need to know who I am. I grew up in a cottage on my uncle's estate. My mother and I were never welcome there because my uncle didn't get on with my mother and viewed the two of us as freeloaders. I received the same education at the same schools as my cousin but only because my grandmother insisted. This is only my second trip abroad…'

Saif was watching her closely. 'I'm listening…' he told her.

'When I was about fifteen my mother began getting forgetful and confused. Eventually she was diagnosed with early-onset dementia. She was only forty years old.' Tati looked reflective, her eyes darkening with sadness. 'I looked after Mum for as long as I could but eventually she had to go into a nursing home. She's been there for almost six years and it costs a fortune. My uncle pays for her care—'

'Which is why you married me,' Saif assumed, slashing ebony brows drawing together in a frown. 'So that you could take care of her yourself.'

'I didn't receive that dowry for marrying you or whatever it's called,' Tati told him immediately. 'My uncle got that. He has debts to settle. That was why Ana was originally willing to marry you, because she has never worked and she's reliant on an income from her father.'

'So, what changed?' Saif pressed.

'Out of the blue, her ex got back in touch and asked her to marry him on the phone while she was here. That's why she ran back to England at the very last minute, leaving me to face the music… She asked me to pretend I was her to give her enough time to leave Alharia. She was afraid her parents would try to prevent her going. I really didn't enjoy deceiving your relatives into believing I was the bride, but I didn't truthfully expect any lasting harm to come from my pretence. I certainly *didn't* realise that I would end up married to you instead!'

'Then why did you agree?' Saif asked bluntly.

'Uncle Rupert threatened to stop paying my mother's nursing home bills. I couldn't let that happen,' Tati murmured heavily. 'She's happy and settled where she is—well, as happy as she can be anywhere now.'

'Will you excuse me for a moment?' Saif asked tautly as he stood up and left the room.

Out in the hall he pulled out his phone and contacted the private investigation agency he often used in business. He wanted information and he wanted it fast. He needed to know everything there was to know about the woman he had married. Ignorance in such a case was inexcusable and had already got him into trouble. The last-minute exchange of brides had plunged him into a situation in which he was not in control and he refused to allow that state of affairs to continue.

Alone in the dining room, Tati felt like dropping her head into her hands and screaming out loud. Why had she told him all that personal stuff? What was the point? She might even be giving him information about herself that he could use as another weapon against her. Saif was not a man she could trust. She cringed at the recollection of what she had said about herself, as if she was apologising for who and what she was, as if she was openly admitting that she was something less than he was just because she hadn't been born into either wealth or status.

Her pride flared at that lowering image and it shamed her, even more than he had already shamed her with that outrageous shopping trip. She had fallen head first into that nasty trap, she conceded painfully.

As Saif strolled back into the room, dark head high, green eyes glinting with assurance, Tati's small hands flexed into claws, that family trait of violence he had accused her of harbouring leaping through her instantaneously. 'You sent me out shopping so that you could snigger behind my back when I met all your worst expectations!' she condemned furiously. 'And I was mad enough at you to allow you to goad me into behaving badly!'

'I don't know what you're talking about,' Saif countered with unblemished cool. 'I do not snigger.'

Pansy-blue eyes now as hard as diamond cutters, Tati tossed her head back, soft, full mouth rigid. 'I'm done with talking to you. I'm done with telling you the truth and letting you judge me for what I can't help or change. You set me up to get me out of your hair and to make a fool of myself and I played right into your hands!' she condemned.

'I didn't set you up when I sent you shopping,' Saif retorted crisply. 'I arranged the outing to entertain you.'

'Like hell you did!' Tati raged back at him.

'And if you played right into my hands, surely that is your own fault?' Saif drawled smoothly.

'Oh, you…*you*…!' The exclamation was framed between gritted teeth. Tati's hands knotted into fists because she wanted to swear at him and she didn't swear, not with the memory of her Granny Milly telling her that only people with a weak grasp of language needed to use curse words. 'I've never been in shops that exclusive in my life. I've never owned clothing such as I'm wearing now. I went shopping to punish you.'

'Why would you have wanted to punish me?' he enquired in wonderment.

'I thought you deserved to have a spendthrift wife after labelling me a gold digger! I know it doesn't sound like much of a punishment right now but at the time...*at the time*...it made sense to me,' she confided in an angry challenge that dared him to employ logic against her. 'But then I got tempted by all those beautiful fabrics and designs and how I looked in them. I started to actually enjoy myself... and I'll never *ever* forgive you for that, for tempting me into wasting all that money.'

'I arranged for you to go out shopping and I would not describe the outfit you are currently wearing as a waste on any level,' Saif asserted softly. 'You look amazing in it.'

'And do you seriously think that *your* opinion makes any difference to the way I feel?' Tati flung back at him furiously. 'Well, it doesn't! I hardly brought any clothes with me to Alharia. Why would I have? As far as I knew I was only staying for forty-eight hours and I certainly didn't factor in marrying you and being swept off to Paris!'

'In other words, you *needed* to go shopping,' Saif interpreted with an unshakeable calm that simply sent her temperature rocketing again because it was infuriating that the more she freaked out, the calmer he became. 'I don't understand why you're so upset.'

'Because I could have bought ordinary cheap clothes and proved to you that I'm *not* a greedy gold digger!' Tati yelled back at him.

'You're my wife and entitled to a decent wardrobe. I wouldn't want you swanning round in what you describe as "cheap" clothes,' Saif pointed out with distaste.

'For heaven's sake, I'm not your wife!' Tati fired back at him in vehement disagreement.

'From the instant you shared that bed with me, and an annulment became an impossibility, you also became my wife in law *and* in my eyes,' Saif informed her with fierce conviction. 'You were a virgin. While you urged me not to make a fuss about that fact, it did make a difference on my terms. Perhaps that is old-fashioned of me, but you do now feel very much like my wife and all this nonsense about how much you spend on the clothes you needed is pointless now.'

'I'm not your wife,' Tati argued in a low, tight voice. 'If you wanted an annulment to end this marriage then you didn't want a wife and we could still apply for an annulment. We could *lie*.'

Her prince threw his handsome dark head back and surveyed her with narrowed, glittering green eyes. 'I do not tell lies of that nature and, now that the marriage has been consummated, neither will you. For the moment, we will make the best of our situation until such time as our circumstances change and we are free to go our separate ways. In the meantime, you are entitled to a very healthy allowance as my wife and I will take over the cost of your mother's nursing care, so let us have no more foolish talk about how you shouldn't spend *my* money.'

'I would lie to get an annulment,' Tati told him stubbornly. 'I don't normally tell lies but in this instance I would be prepared to lie… Just putting that out there for you to consider.'

'I have considered it and I reject it,' Saif stated curtly. 'I—'

'No, there's no need for another moral lecture,' Tati hastened to assure him. 'I do know the difference between right and wrong but I *also* know that neither of us *freely* agreed to marry the other.'

'And yet you gave your virginity to me.'

Tati's face burned red as fire. 'I didn't give you anything… Well, I did, but not the way you make it sound! I was attracted to you and we had sex. Let's leave it there.'

'But where *does* that leave us exactly?' Saif demanded impatiently.

Tati winced at his persistence. 'You can't put a label on everything.'

'I need to know where I stand with you,' Saif breathed with driving emphasis. 'You have to put *some* kind of label on us.'

'Friends…hopefully eventually,' Tati suggested weakly. 'Maybe friends with benefits. Wouldn't that be the best description?'

In the tense silence that gradually stretched, a slow-burning smile slowly wiped the raw tension from Saif's expressive mouth and his vaguely confrontational stance eased. His extraordinary eyes clung to her blushing face. 'Yes. I could work with that,' he murmured in a husky tone of acceptance. 'Yes, I could definitely work within those parameters.'

'I'm really sleepy,' Tati mumbled, putting a hand to her mouth as if to politely screen a yawn, a potent mix of embarrassment and confusion assailing her. 'May we call a halt to the post-mortem for now?'

'It's been a long day,' Saif agreed, deciding to look into whether or not that phrase 'friends with benefits' encompassed what he thought it did.

Naturally, he had heard the expression before. He knew there was a movie by that name but he had never watched it and had never entertained the concept of attempting so spontaneous and casual a relationship with any woman. Although he was close to some of his female cousins, he was mindful of his position and there was no one in whom he confided. He had only once had a female friend. He had been a student at the time and his supposed female friend had suddenly announced that she was in love with him and everything had become horribly awkward from that point on. His sole sexual outlet was occasional one-night stands and that kind of informal never led to a misunderstanding.

At the same time, he marvelled at his bride's audacity in making such a suggestion. He had always assumed that there was truth in that old chestnut that women generally wanted more than sex and friendship from a man, but obviously there were exceptions to every rule. Possibly his own outlook was a little out of date, he thought uneasily, wondering darkly if his father's rigidly traditional attitudes could have coloured his views more than he was willing to admit. Even so, if he and his bride had no choice but to remain together for the present, why shouldn't they make the best of it in and out of the bedroom?

Bearing in mind his distrust of committed relationships, formed by his inability to forget how easily his mother had walked away from him and his father, he suspected that being friends with benefits might be an excellent recipe for temporary intimacy.

Tati sped back upstairs as if she were being chased because she was reeling in shock from what she had accidentally said to Saif, and the manner in which he had received what had undoubtedly struck him as an *invitation*. Her face burned afresh as she got ready for bed, every movement reminding her of what had occurred earlier because the ache of her first sexual experience still lingered with tingling awareness. And, strangely, so did the hot curling sensation she experienced deep down inside whenever she thought about it.

Not strange, she adjusted, simply normal. There was nothing weird about sexual chemistry and Saif had buckets of sex appeal. Even moving across the room, all loose-limbed grace and earthy masculinity, he entrapped her gaze and when she collided with those startling green eyes of his she felt lightheaded. So, no mystery there about what had led to her downfall, she told herself plainly. She had never been affected like that by a man before, certainly not to the extent that he interfered with her brain and her wits and smashed through her every defence.

She even *said* the wrong things around Saif, she acknowledged unhappily. She had been desperate to hide how deeply affected she had been by their intimacy, desperate to keep up an impenetrable front. After all, Saif had taken the sex in his stride without betraying any emotional reaction whatsoever. She had wanted it to look as though she took such steps with equally bold panache, so she had seized on the chance the friends idea offered with alacrity and had added in that ghastly *benefits* tag to coolly attempt to dismiss the reality that they had already got far more familiar than mere friendship allowed. She had been referring to the past, *not* to the potential future. Was it any wonder that he had seemingly got the wrong message? And was she planning to disabuse him of the idea that she was willing to continue their relationship as a friend with benefits?

Her head beginning to ache with her ever-circling thoughts and a growing sense of panic that she had let her life get so out of control when she was normally a very calm and organised person, Tati slid into bed, convinced that she had not a prayer of sleeping. And yet moments later, odd as it seemed to her the following morning, sheer emotional and physical exhaustion sent her crashing straight into a deep sleep.

Saif went to bed in a totally distracted manner far from his usual style. His wife, that much-maligned bride of his, had without warning become a *real* wife. It might be a casual bond, it might not be destined to last for very long, but he was much inclined to believe, even though he had yet to receive concrete facts in an investigation file, that Tatiana was telling him the truth about herself.

Saif was a shrewd observer and he trusted his own instincts. His assumptions about her had been laid down from Dalil Khouri's first reference to her as a fortune hunter, an adventuress, a gold-digging socialite with expensive tastes, who could find no wealthier husband than a Middle Eastern prince from an oil-rich country like Alharia. That might well be true of the woman he *should* have married, the one they called Ana. She was the daughter of the grasping uncle and aunt. He had himself witnessed their threatening behaviour towards their niece with their

raised hands, angry voices and devious looks, he
conceded grimly. Now he believed that those original allegations were *not* true of the woman he had
actually married.

The very beautiful, sensual woman he had married, Saif repeated inwardly as he glanced at her,
sound asleep on the pillow beside his, long wheaten
hair tumbled across the linen, soft pink mouth relaxed, porcelain skin flushed. He had stayed up late
watching *that* film. It had struck him as fashionable
and he didn't do, or certainly never before had done,
'fashionable.' But the creeping, unpleasant suspicion
that he could be as much of a dyed-in-the-wool tradi-
tionalist as his father, unable to adapt to the modern
world or to a modern woman, had cut through him
like a knife and hammered his pride.

So, although it went against his *every* instinct,
Saif was determined to do the 'friends with benefits'
thing even though the movie had already demon-
strated the pitfalls. After all, he would not be emo-
tionally vulnerable, would he? He did not have the
habit of attachment, he reasoned with resolve, he had
never been in a proper relationship and had always
kept his distance from that level of involvement. He
would not be guilty of attaching feelings to sex. He
knew all about sex. They would be friends, *sexual*
friends. A pulse beat at his groin stirred at the mere
thought of repeating that encounter with her.

Even so, he would exercise caution, he told himself fiercely, scrutinising her delicate profile and feathery eyelashes, noting the tiny group of freckles scattered across her nose, the gentle curve of her pink lips. He wanted to see her smile for a change. And why not? She was his wife, deserving of respect and consideration, regardless of how casual and temporary their alliance was. He might not be cutting-edge trendy, as she appeared to be, but he believed that with the exercise of a little imagination and research, he knew how to treat a woman well...

CHAPTER SIX

TATI STUMBLED AS she walked away from the giant
Ferris wheel on the Place de la Concorde. Her head
was still spinning from the experience and the fabulous views of Paris. Saif's hand shot out to steady
her and she glanced up at him with a huge grin. 'My
goodness…that was amazing!' she exclaimed.

Saif gazed down into her glowing face and the
bright blue eyes lit up with enjoyment and he bent
his head and crushed her mouth hungrily under his.
That hunger speared through Tati like a flame striking touchpaper. Her knees wobbled and her hands
closed into his sleeves to keep her upright. The ur-
gent plunge of his tongue formed a pool of liquid
heat in her pelvis and she gasped.

Saif jerked his head up, momentarily disconcerted
to discover that he was in a public place, his bodyguards all politely looking away and probably as-
tonished by his behaviour. In the crush of tourists
and cameras flashing, he clenched his jaw hard. A

very faint darkening scored his high cheekbones as he closed a hand over his wife's and walked her in the direction of the picnic lunch awaiting them on the Champ de Mars. He felt vaguely as though she had intoxicated him.

'The Louvre was exhausting.' Tati sighed as she sank down on the rugs already laid across the springy grass for their comfort. She imagined that going sightseeing with Saif was very different from the usual tourist trek. They didn't queue, they didn't wait anywhere for anything and everything that they required was instantly provided. Her elegant black sundress pooled around her feet and she tugged off her high heels to curl bare pink toes into the grass beyond the rug.

'We did only do the highlights tour. I spent months working in Paris and I went to the Louvre several times,' Saif imparted with amusement, watching the way the sunshine bathed her luxuriant mane of hair in gold. He wanted to touch her again and the temptation entertained him because it was a novelty.

Usually, one taste of a woman was sufficient for him and he would move on. Sex, however, was a great leveller, Saif allowed cynically and, clearly, he hadn't enjoyed enough of it for too long because around Tatiana he was on the constant edge of arousal and it was a challenge to resist her appeal. Yet, only a few yards away, young lovers were lying in the grass kissing passionately with their bodies entwined and their mouths mashed together. The Crown Prince of Alharia, however, had always known that he was not able to practise that kind of freedom and he told himself that he was too disciplined to give way to so juvenile a display. Yet he had kissed her in the street, utterly forgetting where he was, *who* he was.

'I'm not really into art. Mum was,' Tati confided. 'She could look at a picture and make those high-brow comments the way people do, but then she went to art college and originally planned to train as an art historian.'

Dainty little bites of food were set out on a low table in front of them along with china plates and wine glasses in an elaborate spread.

In terms of an outside space, it was a picnic, but not quite the kind of picnic Tati had naïvely envis-aged when Saif had first mentioned it. The Prince, she was starting to realise, didn't truly know what informal or casual was. He was far too accustomed to top-flight silent service. Marcel had arrived laden down with hampers and his spry companion, who was an Alharian, had served them, moving forward on his knees with a bent head as though even to meet the eyes of the Emir's heir would be a familiarity too far. A lot of people were watching the display but Saif seemed no more aware of that scrutiny than of the presence of the plain-clothes police hovering beyond the ring of their personal protection team, keeping a watchful eye over a foreign royal. But then why would he be aware? she asked herself ruefully. Presumably, this was Saif's world as it always was, surrounded by security and hemmed in by tradition and formality.

'Why didn't *you* go to college?' Saif asked softly.

'Further education wasn't an option for me after Granny died. Uncle Rupert was covering the cost of the nursing home and I was already living below their roof because, when Mum went into care, my uncle needed to rent out the cottage we had been using to set against the bills and I was too young to live alone,' Tati explained wryly. 'I felt obligated to help around the house because they couldn't afford full-time staff and I was able to plug the gaps.'

'Your relatives should not have allowed you to make such a sacrifice,' Saif opined, impressed by the sacrifices she had made on her mother's behalf. When he had been younger, he had been much more curious about his absent mother, particularly after her death. He might even have initially sought out his brother to find out more about the woman who had brought him into the world and then walked away. Angel had told him all he needed to know about his absent parent, had satisfied that empty space inside him.

'She's my mother and she was a loving one. It was my duty to do what I could to pay my uncle back,' Tati contradicted gently. 'If I'd gone to college I would have built up thousands of pounds in student loans and it would have been years before I was in a position to make a decent financial contribution. I'm only twenty-one. I've still got loads of time to study and focus on a career.'

'That was a mature decision,' Saif acknowledged, wryly recalling the party girl he had assumed he was marrying while conceding that, undeniably, her cousin made a far more appropriate wife for a man in his position.

Tati nibbled at the delicious finger food on the plates and quaffed her wine.

'We have one personal topic which we haven't yet but *must* touch on,' Saif murmured in a low voice, and he topped up her wine glass, impervious to the shocked appraisal of the server hovering only yards away, keen to jump at the smallest sign of either of them having any need for attention.

Smooth brow furrowing, Tati glanced at him, thinking how incredibly good-looking he was with sunshine gleaming off his black hair and olive skin, lighting his eyes to a sea-glass green shade. 'And what is that?' she prompted abstractedly.

'Yesterday I was negligent in my care of you. As the experienced partner, all the blame on that score is mine. But that recklessness must not be repeated. In our position, the potential consequences would bring complications we would not want to deal with,' Saif framed in a taut undertone of warning.

It took a rather long moment for Tati to grasp

what he was talking about. *'Negligent in my care of you...consequences...complications...mustn't be repeated...'* And then the penny of comprehension dropped with a resounding thump and her tummy curdled in dismay. He was referring to their lack of contraceptive common sense the day before. What else could he be talking about? He hadn't used birth control and she had reassured him, it only occurring to her later that her contraception was scarcely reliable when she had already been off it for a couple of days because she had left her strip of pills behind in England. Losing the rosy colour in her cheeks, she paled and swallowed down her misgivings before sipping her wine while studiously not looking in *his* direction.

There was no point worrying him ahead of time when really...what were the chances that she would conceive the very *first* time she had sex? She gritted her teeth, anxiety flashing through her as she reminded herself that she was not a naïve teenager, thinking that that should be sufficient to keep her safe. There was a chance, *of course*, there was when, even with precautions, no form of contraception was foolproof.

'We need to be responsible,' she said, proud of the steadiness of her voice until it occurred to her that, once again, she was throwing up a green light for further such intimacy.

And she shouldn't be doing that, of course, she

shouldn't be. Even though she had *enjoyed* the experience? Her cheeks hot, she argued with herself inside her head. If they were careful going forward, there was no reason why she shouldn't be intimate with Saif again. She was an adult woman capable of making that choice on her own behalf. There was nothing morally wrong about having a sexual relationship, she reminded herself irritably, as long as the same consequences that had derailed her mother's life did not assail her.

Sadly, unplanned pregnancies sometimes extracted the highest price from the female partner, she reflected ruefully, because a man might have to contribute to his child's maintenance, but that did not necessarily mean that he took on any share of the childcare or indeed had any further interest in the child involved.

Her father had been of that ilk, indifferent from the day that her mother had informed him of her pregnancy. Even after his release from prison, he had pleaded poverty when pursued by the law for child support payments. She had never met her reluctant father in the flesh. As a teenager she had once written to him asking for a meeting but, even though the courts had verified her paternity, he had only responded with the denial that she was his child. That had hurt, that had blown a giant hole in her secret hope that he was curious about her as well.

'Yes,' Saif agreed, relieved, it seemed, by her attitude, which only made her feel even guiltier for not being fully honest with him from the outset and just admitting that there was a risk, admittedly, she *hoped*, a very slight risk that conception was a possibility.

Only telling the truth would make her sound like such an idiot, she conceded ruefully. She had told him it was safe. She had told him she was on contraception, only to recognise when it was too late that the pill method only worked if taken on a consistent schedule.

'We're attending a party tonight,' Saif murmured, disconcerting her with the ease with which he flipped the topic of conversation. 'You should enjoy it. I believe it's usually quite a spectacle.'

'Fancy, then,' Tati assumed, mentally flipping through her new wardrobe and realising with some embarrassment that she had bought so much that she couldn't remember all of the outfits without the garments being physically in front of her. That was not a problem that she had ever thought she would live to have, she acknowledged ruefully.

'Very,' Saif confirmed lazily, watching her with eyes that were sea-glass bright green seduction in the sunlight, his gaze enhanced by dense black spiky lashes. He wasn't touching her, he didn't *need* to touch her, she acknowledged in wonderment, he just had to look at her a certain way and that certain way was, without a doubt, incredibly sexy and potent.

Heat rose at the heart of her, butterflies fluttering in her tummy. Dragging her gaze from his, she sipped at her wine, reminding herself afresh that she was an adult woman, able to make her own choices… and right now, she thought, dizzy in the grip of that sensual intoxication, her choice was *him*.

Ana had always told Tati that she was very naïve about men. Her cousin prided herself on being as ruthless as any male in taking what she wanted from a man and then moving on, regardless of how the man felt about it. Ana often left broken hearts in her wake. Tati not only didn't *want* to leave broken hearts behind her, but also didn't think she would ever possess the power her cousin seemed to have over the opposite sex.

No, she couldn't compare herself to Ana, Tati acknowledged back at the magnificent house while she browsed through her wide selection of gowns. She was not and would never be a heartbreaker, but she rather suspected that Saif fell into that category. He emanated that cool, sophisticated air of unavailability that her cousin found so attractive in a man, so it was rather ironic that he had ended up married to Tati instead. Tati, unrefined, clumsy…and so angry from the moment he had met her.

Tati had never argued and fought with anyone the way she had with Saif. And where had all that rage come from? She supposed it had built up over the years below her uncle and aunt's roof where she had been consistently bullied and reminded of her lowly place in life on a daily basis. The smallest request for a wage that would at least fund her bus trips to visit her mother and little gifts for the older woman had been viewed as an offence of ingratitude. That she was a 'charity' child dependent on the goodwill of others for survival had been brought home to her hard and often and that label had ground her pride into the dust. Her mother's troubled past, her care bills and even the family embarrassment caused by Tati's illegitimate birth had often been used as a stick to beat Tati with and keep her down. Her uncle would not have dared be so offensive had her mother been around still possessed of her cutting tongue.

At the same time, her grandmother had had no idea what went on in her own house and Tati had shielded the frail old lady from the ugly truth. Even so, her Granny Milly had once taken the trouble to assure Tati that her mother would *always* be looked after, and Tati had prayed that sufficient money would be laid aside in the old lady's will to cover the nursing home costs. Unhappily, though, her late grandmother had forgotten that promise and had remembered neither her daughter Mariana nor Tati in her last will and testament.

That oversight had hurt, Tati conceded ruefully, because she had been deeply attached to her grandmother. In addition, the soothing knowledge that her mother's care was secure would not only have meant the world to Tati, but would also have released her from her virtual servitude in her uncle's home. But she had long since forgiven the old lady, who had been quite ill and confused towards the end of her life.

Shaking her head clear of those disturbing recollections of the past, Tati tugged a silvery-grey evening gown out of one of the closets. The delicate lace overlay was cobweb fine and it shimmered below the lights. She had fallen in love with the elegant dress at first sight, thinking comically that it was a princess dress for a grown-up, it not occurring to her that she was, technically speaking anyway, now a princess, thanks to her marriage to a prince. The modest neckline and long sleeves might not be eye-catching, but the gown had a quiet, stylish elegance that appealed to her.

As she emerged fully clad from the bathroom, her make-up applied in a few subtle touches, Saif stilled halfway out of his shirt. Tati paused as well, reluctantly enthralled by the expanse of muscular bronzed chest on view. He was beautifully built from his broad shoulders to his narrow waist and long, powerful thighs. For a split second she remembered the weight of him over her and she was suddenly so short of breath she almost choked, her cheeks flaming as she coughed and croaked, 'Sorry, wasn't expecting to see you!'

'That dress is spectacular on you,' Saif breathed appreciatively, because that particular shade of grey enhanced the deep blue of her eyes and lent a glow to her porcelain skin while the tailoring of the dress sleekly outlined the feminine curves of her lush figure.

'Seriously?' Tati queried, her head lifting high again.

'Seriously,' he confirmed, strolling across the room to indicate the gift boxes on the highly polished dressing table. 'These are for you.'

'Presents? It's not my birthday yet,' Tati told him, lifting a gift box with the certainty that such packaging could only contain jewellery and uncomfortable at the prospect.

'As my wife, you need to wear jewels. It's expected,' Saif said smoothly.

Tati dealt him a suspicious glance before opening the boxes to reveal a diamond necklace and earrings. 'These are…spectacular,' she whispered truthfully, a fingertip reverently stroking the rainbow fire of a single gleaming gem. 'But I *shouldn't*—'

'No. These are family jewels that my father once gave to my mother. My mother left everything behind when she left Alharia and it would please my father very much to know that his gifts are being worn again.'

'Is your mother still alive?' Tati asked gently, detaching the necklace from the box, feeling the cool of the beautiful gems against her skin as her reluctance to wear the diamonds melted away.

'No, she passed away about three years ago in a helicopter crash with her husband,' Saif explained.

'Did you ever meet her again after she left your father? Or even see her?' she prompted, intrigued by his seemingly calm attitude to his abandonment as a child.

'I was devastated when I heard of her death,' Saif heard himself admit, disconcerting himself almost as much as he surprised Tati with that declaration. 'While she was alive I could toy with the idea of looking her up and getting to know her—should she have been interested—but once she was gone, that possibility was gone for ever.'

'I know what you mean,' Tati murmured wryly. 'I wrote to my father when I was a teenager asking him to meet me and, even though it had been proven in court that I was his daughter, he wrote back telling me that he wasn't my father and didn't wish to hear from me again. It hurt a lot. My mother had tried to warn me that he wasn't interested, but I was too stubborn to listen.'

'My father told me that he didn't think that my mother had many maternal genes. Some women don't, I believe, and presumably fathers can suffer from the same flaw. Let me help,' he murmured, crossing the room to remove the necklace from her fingers and settle it round her throat, his fingertips brushing the nape of her neck as he clasped it, sending a faint quiver of awareness through her.

Awesomely conscious of his proximity and the familiar scent of his cologne, Tati struggled to behave normally as she donned the earrings and finally turned to let him see her.

'Perfect,' Saif pronounced.

'I'll wait downstairs for you,' Tati told him breathlessly, not sure that she could withstand the desire to watch him while he undressed, and mortified by the temptation. It was as though Saif had cast some weird kind of sex spell over her, she conceded shamefacedly as Marcel offered her a drink in the grand main salon.

It was normal, healthy lust, Tati supposed of her fixation and her growing obsession with Saif's extraordinary eyes, Saif's hands, what he could do with them, how it felt when he touched her…

Enough of this nonsense, she mentally screamed at herself. She was behaving with all the maturity of a schoolgirl with a first crush. None of it was any big deal, she told herself bracingly, deciding that she was only so bemused and off balance because she was a decidedly late starter when it came to the opposite sex. All over again, she wished she had acquired some of her cousin's glossy cool and confidence. But, marooned on a country estate without money and with few social outlets, Tati had not enjoyed her cousin's opportunities to meet men and date. In reality, Tati thought with regret, she probably *was* as naïve as an adolescent.

When she climbed into the limo with Saif she was, momentarily, tempted to pinch herself before accepting that the designer gown, the incredibly handsome man by her side and the opulent mode of travel could figure in *her* new lifestyle. It was even more ironic to know that her uncle and aunt would now be furious that *she* was the one benefiting from the marriage rather than their daughter. They had needed her to marry the Prince to gain access to that dowry, but it would still outrage them that their niece was now living in luxury. And for the first time, Tati acknowledged that she was grateful to have escaped her relatives' demands, relieved to know that in many ways she was finally free and that her mother's residence in her care home was secure. She would eventually be able to look towards her own future, unfettered by the limits imposed on her by others.

'You're very quiet this evening,' Saif remarked as they crossed the pavement to the large illuminated mansion with its classic gardens that were equally well-lit to show off glimpses of women in elaborate dresses and men in dinner jackets, their necks craned as they watched the glorious fireworks shooting and sparkling across the night sky in a rainbow of colour and illumination.

'Gosh, these people know how to party,' Tati commented, hugely impressed by her surroundings as they stepped into a brilliantly lit hall and a crush of little groups of chattering people. And everybody, literally *everybody*, looked as though they might be a celebrity of some kind. In such company, neither her gown nor her magnificent diamonds could ever look like overkill. 'Are the hosts close friends of yours?'

'No. I owe this invitation to the relative whose house we are using,' Saif admitted. 'But I have no doubt that I will see familiar faces here.'

'Yes. I suppose you get to meet a lot of people.'

'Because the Emir doesn't travel. I take care of Alharia's diplomatic interests in his place. It entails attending formal receptions and dinners. You'll be accompanying me to some of them,' he declared, startling her.

'Me?' Tati stressed in a low mutter of disconcertion as he curved a guiding hand to her taut spine.

'The joys of marrying a crown prince,' Saif murmured teasingly, his breath fanning her cheekbone. 'Some of that kind of socialising is boring but, equally, sometimes it's fascinating.'

'I should've realised that there would be…er… duties to carry out in this role.' Tati sighed. 'It all happened so fast, though… One minute Ana was running for the airport and the next we were married.'

In the midst of that speech, Saif was hailed by two men, who addressed him in another language. It wasn't French and it wasn't English, and she was introduced and served with a drink of champagne by a passing waiter before they moved on into a room. 'Could we go out and see the fireworks?' she pressed once they were alone again.

Saif glanced down at her in surprise, for in his experience women in their finery avoided the outdoors like the plague. The unhidden eagerness brimming in her upturned gaze, however, made him laugh and for a moment she seemed much younger than her years. 'Why do you want to see them?'

'Mum was so terrified of fireworks that I never got to see them properly as a child. When she was young she witnessed a dreadful accident, which injured a friend at a firework event, and it put her off them for life,' she explained. 'Every Bonfire Night, we sat indoors with the curtains closed and then, the next day, Ana would tell me how much fun she had had at whichever party she had been invited to and I would feel madly jealous.'

Saif's expressive lips quirked. 'Naturally.'

They stood on the paved terrace watching the display until a low murmur of a comment made Tati turn her head. A very tall brunette in a startlingly see-through dress was stalking towards them. For a split second, Tati was guilty of staring, taken aback by a woman revealing that much flesh in public, showing off her bare breasts and her nipple rings below the thin white chiffon gown. Truly, however, Tati was forced to admit, the woman had a *superb* body. In haste she turned her head away from the conspicuous beauty, only to stiffen in astonishment when the woman appeared in front of them and greeted Saif with the kind of familiarity that no woman wanted to see her male companion receive in her presence.

'Saif!' she carolled, followed by a voluble gush of French as she walked her long, manicured fingertips up over his chest in a very inviting gesture.

'Juliette,' Saif murmured with rather more restraint. 'May I introduce you to my wife, Tatiana?'

'Your *wife*?' Juliette gasped in consternation while walking her fingers down over his flat muscular stomach in unmistakable invitation.

Tati couldn't stop herself. In a knee-jerk reaction, she reached out and pushed the brunette's hand away from Saif. 'His wife, sorry,' she said with a smile that she was sure was unconvincing.

A split second later, Juliette having languorously taken the hint and strolled away, Tati was shattered by her own possessive and wholly inappropriate reaction to another woman touching the man she had married. Saif didn't belong to her in the usual sense of married people. They weren't in love either. She had come up with the label of friends with benefits but even that wasn't a fair tag for them, because people in that kind of relationship were generally those who had had a reasonably long and close friendship before intimacy developed and she and Saif didn't fit into that category either. The intense colour of mortification swept her cheeks and she felt as though she were burning alive inside her own skin.

'I'm sorry… She was annoying me,' she said uncomfortably.

'It was unseemly for her to touch me in that way,' Saif murmured, appraising her with gleaming green eyes fringed by black lashes. 'There is no need for an apology.'

But regardless of what he said, Tati felt very differently. She had shocked herself with that little show of possessive behaviour. After all, she wasn't entitled to be that territorial with Saif. She should not be experiencing any prompting to react as though she were jealous of another woman touching him. Of course, she wasn't jealous or possessive of him, she told herself fiercely.

'And it was sexy,' Saif murmured in a husky undertone, gazing down at her with potent green eyes of appreciation. 'Very, very sexy.'

Stunned, Tati looked back at him in wonderment and then she couldn't help herself—she laughed, and all her discomfiture was washed away as though it had never been. Evidently, Saif took a very different view of her attitude, but as the evening wore on she continued to marvel at the way she had behaved. Clearly, she *was* possessive of Saif. Was that simply because she had gone to bed with him?

Brow furrowing, she attempted, during all the

chatter, the dancing and the eating that comprised the lively party atmosphere, to pin down what she was feeling about the man she had married. It was surprisingly difficult. She had travelled at speed from raging resentment and frustration over her powerlessness to grudging acceptance that Saif had had little more choice than she had in their marriage. And somewhere along the line she had begun lusting after him, *liking* him, appreciating his calm, measured approach to life. It certainly didn't mean that she was developing any kind of mental attachment to him, she assured herself confidently.

She wasn't so naïve that she would confuse lust and love, was she? Admittedly, she was enthralled by the fluid movement of his hips against hers on the dance floor, the pulsing ache building between her thighs and the provocative awareness that she was having the *same* physical effect on him. Unlike her, he couldn't hide his response. She was insanely conscious of his arousal. And that sheer reciprocity thrilled Tati because it made her feel powerful and seductive for the first time in her life, no longer a weak pawn in someone else's game, but an equal. She was finally making her own choices and doing what pleased her, rather than someone else.

'So, you and Juliette?' Tati whispered as she stretched up to Saif. 'Do share…'

Saif tensed, wondering why on earth she would ask such an awkward question before reminding himself that women were often morbidly curious about a man's past. His three older sisters had taught him that, always prying where their interest was least welcome.

'Was she your girlfriend?' Tati prompted.

'No. It was a casual connection.' Saif shrugged in emphasis, hoping that her curiosity concluded there, long brown fingers skimming soothingly down the side of her face. 'I can't keep my hands off you,' he breathed with a sudden raw edge to his dark, deep drawl that sent a responsive shiver of delight down her taut spine.

'It's mutual,' she whispered.

Even so, she was still assailed by a sudden perverse attack of guilt and discomfiture because, try as she might to be a bolder version of her old self, being bold still felt sinful and brazen. She would have to work harder on that outlook, she told herself firmly, because being quiet, accepting and the person others preferred her to be had only served to deprive her of her freedom and her choices in life. Wanting Saif, allowing herself to succumb to that sizzling chemistry that went way beyond anything she had ever experienced, was probably the most daring thing she had ever done. And one of the best things about Saif, Tati reflected happily, was that he hadn't known her as she used to be and, with him, she could be entirely her true self.

He curved an arm round her in the limousine on

the drive back to the house. She was gloriously aware of the strength of his lean, powerful frame up against her and the subtle musky, fragrant scent of him that close. Her heart was pounding in her chest when he stopped on the landing halfway up the fabulous staircase of the town house and hauled her up against him to kiss her with all the fierce hunger she craved. The lancing touch of his tongue inside her mouth set her on fire and a choked moan escaped low in her throat.

Her whole body was surging with wild anticipation and, lifting her, he cannoned into the bedroom, pushing her back against the wall and pinning her there afresh to crush her lips hungrily beneath his again. Her heart was thumping, her pulses thrumming because that rocketing passion of his took her over and thrilled her to death. It was the exact match of her own, a wild, seething need that drove out every other logical thought, leaving only the wanting behind.

Saif turned her round to run down the zip on her dress, pushing it off her shoulders, stroking it down her arms until it dropped round her feet. Kicking off her shoes, heartbeat accelerating, she stepped out of the dress. His lips traced the line of her shoulder and every nerve ending in her body leapt to attention as she pressed back into the heat of him, breathless and boneless with need.

'I like the lingerie,' Saif husked with appreciation as he carefully lifted her and lowered her down onto the well-sprung bed. 'But I think I'll like you even better out of it.'

Flushed and wide-eyed, her eyes very blue in her face, Tati watched Saif shed his tailored dinner jacket and bow tie, standing over her while he unbuttoned his dress shirt, smouldering emerald-green eyes locked to the silvery-grey cobweb-fine bra and panties she sported and the firm, soft curves they enhanced. 'Your eyes are so unusual,' she whispered, and then wanted to cringe at herself for saying it just at that moment.

'As I said, my only inheritance from my mother,' Saif muttered, his shirt fluttering to the floor, exposing an impressive bronzed torso composed of chiselled abs and a flat, taut stomach and the intriguing little furrow of black hair that ran down below his waistband. 'But I didn't like being different as a child when everyone else's eyes were dark. You occasionally see blue eyes in the desert tribes but never this shade.'

Something clenched almost painfully in Tati's stomach as she looked up at him. He came down on the bed beside her, naked and aroused and, oh, so sexy to her riveted gaze. 'I *like* your eyes,' she framed unevenly, her chest lifting as she dragged in a sustaining breath.

His expert mouth toyed with hers while he released her bra and explored the pouting swells and hard tips eager for his attention. He trailed his lips down to tease those rosy, sensitive crowns and her hips rose and she gasped, her entire body shimmying on an edge of gathering anticipation, desire twisting sharp as a knife inside her, tensing every muscle. He skimmed away the panties, parted her thighs and she trembled, feeling shy, tempted to say no but too aroused to have that discipline.

And then he employed his tongue on her and exquisite sensation flooded her. He dipped a finger into her tight channel and her spine arched, the craving climbing again. Melting heat liquefied her pelvis, excitement gripping her taut, and before she could even work out what was happening to her, she became a creature only capable of response, so worked up to a peak that she could only moan and gasp while her body moved in a compulsive rhythm. When she reached a climax it was fast and furious, ripping through her quivering length in an explosion of raw heat and ecstasy, leaving her flopping back against the pillows, limp as a noodle.

Saif dug into the cabinet beside the bed and donned protection. 'We will take no further risks,' he murmured with a slanting, charismatic smile.

Relief filled Tati because she had been thinking that perhaps she ought to go out and look for an English-speaking doctor and ask for replacement pills. But wouldn't Saif's precautions be sufficient until she went back to England to see her mother and reclaimed her possessions from her uncle's home?

Convinced that she no longer needed to worry on that score, Tati wrapped her arms round him as he came down to her again. Her body was still pulsing with the aftermath of satiation and highly sensitive.

'I've been thinking about this moment all day and all evening,' Saif groaned, startling green eyes alight with desire.

'*All* day?'

'Yes.'

'Then why did we wait this long?' she whispered as he shifted against her tender core, sliding into her in a sure rocking motion that sent her heart rate flying.

'You tell me,' Saif urged thickly, awash with surprise at the sheer mutuality of sex with Tatiana.

With a twist of his lean hips he pushed deep and fast into the tight, damp welcome awaiting him and he listened with satisfaction to his bride moan with a pleasure that only echoed his own.

His hard, insistent rhythm enthralled her in the wild ride that followed. Excitement roared higher for her with his every thrust. She moved against him, lost in the experience as her excitement rose higher and higher, the need tugging at her every sense pushing her to a frenzied peak where only mindless sensation controlled her. When the glorious wave of excitement tipped her over the edge, she cried out in writhing delight before the last of her energy drained away, leaving her limp and winded.

Saif thrust away the bedding and fell back from her. 'I'm hot...'

Tati grinned and rolled closer, a possessive hand smoothing down over his heaving chest. 'Yes, *very* hot.'

Saif sat up and pulled her to him. 'And you're joining me in the shower.'

'Why? I'm not fit for anything else right now,' she protested, shy about getting out of bed naked in front of him and knowing how silly that was after what they had shared.

'I'm not ready to let go of you yet,' Saif told her truthfully, his fertile imagination already arranging her in erotic positions round the marble bathroom and seeing possibilities everywhere. *Cool off*, his brain told him, *step back, regain control*, because he suddenly felt as though he were in dangerous territory, a territory without rules or boundaries and not his style at all.

That uneasy feeling, that sense of wrong, stabbed at him because Saif liked everything laid out neat and tidy, nothing left to chance. And yet here he was with a wife who wasn't a genuine wife, a lover who wasn't a simple lover and a friend who wasn't a real friend. Where was he supposed to go next? What was his end goal?

And even though Tati knew in her heart of hearts that she shouldn't go there, she was too curious to silence the question brimming on her lips. 'And when will you be ready?'

Having switched on the shower, Saif swung back to her, startlingly handsome with his black hair tousled, his green eyes very shrewd, sharp and bright, his strong jawline defined by black stubble. 'Ready for what?' he queried.

'Ready to let me go?' she almost whispered in daring clarification, sliding past him to take refuge behind the tiled shower wall where he could no longer see her.

Saif froze. 'You're asking how soon we can decently go for a divorce without unduly surprising anyone?' he murmured flatly, unprepared for that sudden far-reaching question and wishing she hadn't asked before he had even had the time to decide on the wisest approach to their predicament. 'Possibly six months…a year? I don't really know yet. We *should* make it look as though we've given the marriage a fair chance before throwing in the cards.'

Six months to a year, Tati mused, thinking what a very short space of time that was. A mere blink and their relationship would be over, done and dusted, ready for the archives. Her tummy hollowed out and sank while she busied herself washing her hair, her movements slowing as she became aware of the little muscles she had strained and the ache between her thighs, the inescapable reminders of their intimacy. Friends with benefits, she reminded herself doggedly, but that tag no longer enjoyed the same exhilarating ring of daring that it had first seemed to have. Indeed, all of a sudden that style of thinking seemed a little sad and immature, she acknowledged ruefully. Saif was making it very clear that what they currently had was a casual fling with an ending scripted in advance.

An ending written and decided at the same instant they had married, she reminded herself. There was nothing personal about his decision, she reasoned, determined not to take umbrage. Saif could never have planned to stay married long-term to the bride his father had picked for him and she could hardly blame him for that, could she? Saif was way too sophisticated to settle for an arranged marriage with a stranger. And when the stranger was also an unsuitable foreigner, a divorce was a fairly predictable conclusion.

Of course, *she* wanted a divorce as well, Tati assured herself. Naturally, she wanted to reclaim her own life again. Yet it was a challenge for Tati to consider a future that she had never been free to consider before. And *would* she be free?

After all, for how long would her marriage to Saif ensure that her uncle would continue paying her mother's expenses? Now that he had got the money he wanted, it was difficult to have faith in the older man's word. Perhaps her mother *would* eventually have to be moved to a cheaper care facility, Tati reasoned unhappily. Beggars couldn't be choosers. There were worse options, she reminded herself impatiently. Whatever happened, she would handle it and she would help her mother to handle it too. Although, had Saif meant it when he had said that from now on *he* would handle her mother's care bills? But, for how long would he be prepared to do that? Would there be a divorce settlement that covered that need?

Tomorrow, she decided, she would phone the nursing home to check on the older woman. She would also ring her mother's cousin, Pauline, who lived only yards from the care facility and who, as Mariana's only other visitor, always had a more personal take on Mariana's condition. She would discuss the possibility of a move with Pauline.

How could she possibly accept *more* money from Saif? Neither she nor her mother were his responsibilities. They could not acknowledge on the one hand that theirs was not a real marriage and then behave as though it were when it came to money. She had to grow up and stop looking to other people to support her, Tati told herself in exasperation. Saif didn't owe her anything!

CHAPTER SEVEN

ALMOST THREE WEEKS into their stay, the bridal couple
were viewing the catacombs beneath Paris.

Saif was uncomfortable with his surroundings. He
had done all the tourist stuff without complaint for
his wife's benefit. He had taken her for a cruise on
the Seine and they had climbed the Eiffel Tower at
night when it was an illuminated beacon of golden
light across the city. He had even dutifully snacked
on macarons at the famous Ladurée, while treach-
erously thinking that they could not match similar
Alharian delicacies. But the catacombs were proving
a step too far for him because he felt claustrophobic
below the low ceilings, and the skulls and remains of
six million souls stacked up to make artistic patterns
in the walls did not improve his mood. Tatiana might
enjoy the morbid atmosphere, but it spooked him.

Tati sidled up behind Saif, forcing his bodyguards
to back away, and stretched up to cover his eyes with

her hands. 'I'm a zombie… *Run!*' she whispered in the creepiest voice she could contrive.

Saif whirled round and gazed down into her lovely smiling face as she giggled, eyes dancing with mischief. It was one of those occasions when she made him feel twice her age, yet it was also one of those times he cherished because she brightened his days like sunshine while simultaneously turning the darker hours into sensual experiences of indescribable pleasure. He valued a bride, blessed with such advantages, obviously he valued her greatly.

That wasn't something he thought about much, though, because she had been with him round the clock since their marriage. He did know, however, that he wasn't looking forward to her departure the following day for a trip back to England to see her mother. She had refused the offer of his company, saying it was unnecessary. He should have been relieved by that breezy dismissal because he had a duty to return to Alharia and see his own parent, not to mention needing to deal with at least a dozen tasks he had been unable to tackle from a distance. For the first time he was acknowledging how much he missed his father and how lucky he had been in the older man's reliable care. Yet Tati's regular references to her mother and her deep attachment to her often made him wonder what he had missed out on.

As a further complication for Saif, there were the worrying irregularities uncovered by the investigation agency he had initially hired to provide him with a background check on his bride. As yet he had no idea what those anomalies meant, and he didn't want to upset Tatiana with concerns that might yet prove to be groundless. He wished to handle that matter in person, rather than allow a member of his staff to deal with such a confidential matter, but if the agency's suspicions *were* true, there *would* be criminal charges brought, he thought with angry disgust.

'Sometimes…you are way too serious,' Tati scolded softly, a fingertip gently tracing the firm sculpted line of his full lower lip.

'But I have you to remind me of the lighter side of life,' Saif countered, closing an arm round her to move her on. 'Let's get out of here…we're eating out tonight.'

'It's sort of our last night,' Tati muttered abstract-edly, small fingers toying with the magnificent emer-ald that hung on a chain round her slender neck as they emerged back into the sunshine, the light momentarily blinding her.

Saif had somehow contrived to talk her out of re-turning to England the week before and she wasn't quite sure how he had done it, because she did miss that regular connection with her mother, slender though it was. It was true that her mother didn't look for her if she was absent. Indeed, Mariana had to be introduced to her daughter at every visit because she no longer recognised her. The time for producing the family photo albums and reminding Mariana was long past because it only confused and upset the older woman now to be confronted with faces and events she had forgotten. So, Tati was accustomed to a mother who greeted her each time as a stranger. And every time, it broke her heart a little more.

For dinner, she picked a dress from her array of choices that she had been saving for a special occasion. It was a cerise-pink print with slender straps and that whole summery vibe somehow encapsulated the holiday spirit of freedom that she had revelled in since her arrival in Paris. Saif, she thought ruefully, really knew how to show a woman a good time. Although he spent several hours a day working, he had devoted more time to ensuring that she enjoyed herself. And whether they had been admiring the gorgeous cathedral of Sainte-Chapelle or wandering hand in hand around Saint-Germain-des-Prés, where she had explored intriguing little shops full of wonders or sat outside cafés watching the world go by, Saif had made a praiseworthy and highly successful effort to entertain her. She had gathered a handful of little gifts that would make her mother's eyes sparkle but she felt guilty as hell for not returning sooner to England.

She had worried too when she hadn't heard anything more from Ana and her texts had failed to receive a response. She was beginning to suspect that the beach wedding that her cousin had been so excited about hadn't happened because Ana documented the big moments in her life with photos and she would definitely have sent at least one photo. Sadly, Tati was reluctant to contact her uncle and aunt to check on Ana's well-being because of the way they had behaved at the wedding in Alharia. She would be staying in a hotel near the care home because she wasn't sure that her relatives would even be willing to offer her hospitality.

'I'll have to pack up and collect my stuff from my uncle's house while I'm in England,' she sighed over dinner in a sophisticated bistro in possession of several Michelin stars that evening.

'No, that would be unwise. You should *avoid* visiting Fosters Manor,' Saif startled her by intoning with a harsh edge of warning to his dark drawl.

'Why on earth would you say that?'

Saif studied her. She was pretty as a picture in her dress, blond hair gleaming below the low lights, soft blue eyes politely enquiring, so naturally lively that she exuded a positive glow of vibrance, but she was also so trusting that she would be innately vulnerable to anyone wishing her ill.

As Saif looked, a stab of lust pulsed in his groin and he almost winced at his own predictability. *That* was beginning to bother him and make him think that the absence of his bride for a week would do him good. He couldn't afford to want Tatiana too much or too often, nor could he allow himself to de-

pend on her for anything when she was only passing
through his life. It was the first time he had ever had
a longer, more intimate relationship with a woman
and he told himself that it was excellent practice for
the future when he would surely find a more lasting partner. Unhappily, however, Tatiana, with all
her little individual quirks and inherent sensuality,
didn't feel like a practice run for *any* other woman.
Even so, he knew that he didn't have Tatiana to keep
and he acted accordingly.

'Why did you say that?' Tati pressed again, her
smooth brow furrowing.

'Your uncle and aunt are hostile towards you, and
I don't trust them,' Saif told her truthfully.

'You think they might murder me and bury me
below the floorboards?' Tati teased.

'Safety concerns are not a joke, Tatiana,' Saif
sliced back, pushing away his serving of Baba au
Rhum with a frown as his appetite died. 'If you *do*
choose to visit your relatives, keep your bodyguards
with you at all times. But there is no need for you to
visit their home merely to collect your possessions.
That can be arranged for you.'

'I don't want my aunt Elizabeth going through my
belongings,' Tati said with distaste. 'And that's what
would happen if I don't go myself. Are you serious
about bodyguards accompanying me to England?'

'Of course. You are my wife, the Crown Princess
of Alharia, and as such require security measures,'

Saif parried without hesitation. 'It's not as though you wear a label saying that you are not my "real" wife, as you are so fond of telling me…or as though anyone wishing me harm would even believe that.'

Tati reddened and shifted uncomfortably in her chair. That was a comment she had regularly made as much for her own benefit as his, because there had been several occasions of late when she had felt that they had crossed boundaries that she had not foreseen at the outset of their agreement. For a start, Saif could not be dissuaded from buying her gifts, not least the huge emerald currently nestling above her breasts.

He seemed to be the sort of guy who liked to buy things for women, and time and time again he had surprised her. She had a gorgeous silk scarf that had cost the earth, designer shoes that looked as though they had been sprinkled with stardust and a diamond bracelet that was blinding in daylight. On her twenty-second birthday, he had engulfed her in gifts and treats and that lavish desire to spoil her rotten had touched her to the heart. There had been a whole host of presents from flowers to little trinkets she had admired. He was ridiculously generous and totally out of touch with what being friends with benefits should encompass—that being, in her view, a much looser and more casual connection.

Only she could hardly criticise Saif when she had been shamelessly, wantonly hogging his attention whenever she got the opportunity. There was nothing casual about her behaviour, she allowed guiltily. They had had sex on his office desk the day before because she was turning into a stage five clinger who found it hard to keep her distance when he was working for several hours.

'Will you promise me that you will be careful of your security while you are away from me?' Saif pressed gravely. 'Even though you think that my concern is unnecessary.'

Tati nodded hurriedly, disconcerted by his reading her so accurately, something he often did and which she found unnerving. The sea-glass brilliance of his eyes made warmth pool in her pelvis, sent her pulse racing, made it difficult for her to catch her breath.

'You haven't eaten much this evening,' Saif commented.

'I probably ate too much all day,' Tati quipped, reluctant to explain the very slight sense of nausea that had afflicted her when the scent of meat assailed her nostrils. She wasn't actually sick and didn't think that she was falling ill, but her usual enthusiasm for food had recently dwindled. Possibly it was the result of eating too many rich, elaborate meals, she reflected ruefully, thinking how easily she had become accustomed to being thoroughly spoiled on the gastronomic front. Now she was clearly getting fussy, craving salad when there were barely any cold options on offer.

An hour later, she walked into the dressing room off their bedroom to check the case she had already partially packed.

'The staff could have taken care of this,' Saif told her from the doorway, moving forward to glance down into the case with a frown. 'You don't seem to be taking very much.'

'At most I'll be away a week and I won't be going any place where I need to dress up,' Tati proffered.

A week. A kind of relief engulfed Saif. A week was no time for a man accustomed to living without a woman although it was astonishing, he acknowledged, how quickly he had become used to her presence and how rarely she irritated him. He was reserved, a loner, and had always suspected that marriage would be a challenge for him, but Tatiana was accepting rather than demanding and took him as he was. He ran an appreciative fingertip over the porcelain pale expanse of her back, caressing the soft silky skin.

'Need some help getting out of this?' Saif husked, tugging on the strap of the dress.

Tati stifled a grin. 'Go ahead…'

The zip went down, and the dress floated to her feet. She stepped unhurriedly out of her heels, super-aware of the fine turquoise silk bra and panties she wore and the intensity of Saif's appraisal. When she glanced up, his stunning green eyes glittered like emeralds and butterflies took flight in her tummy, her body's programmed response to that appreciation as natural as her need to breathe.

Lifting her out of the folds of cloth on the floor, he pinned her slight body to his, a large masculine hand splayed across her bottom to hold her close. His tailored trousers could not hide the hard heat of his erection, and as she felt the raw promise of him against her stomach, fierce desire flashed through her like a storm warning. Her arms snapped round his neck as his mouth came crashing down on hers with a ravaging, smouldering hunger that matched her own.

Somewhere in the background a vaguely familiar snatch of music was playing, and her brain strove to rise to alert status again. There was a reason why she should know that sound, only it didn't seem important with her fingers raking through Saif's silky black hair while her heart was racing and her body was pulsing with insane arousal. He was tumbling her down on the bed with scant ceremony when she realised that that sound was her mobile phone ringing and that there were very good reasons why she always leapt to answer it on the rare occasion that it rang. Consternation gripping her, Tati broke free of that kiss and rolled over, almost falling off the bed in her haste to reach her clutch bag and the phone within it.

Half-naked, she sat on the floor clutching the silent phone and checked the call that she had missed.

It was from her mother's nursing home as she had feared. Within the space of a minute she was ringing back, identifying herself, listening with an anxious expression to what the manager was telling her and asking apprehensive questions, all beneath Saif's frowning gaze. Assuring the older woman that she would be returning to England as soon as she could arrange it, she sat silent, tears prickling her eyes and stinging them before slowly overflowing to drip down her cheeks.

'I should have gone back last week. I should have known better. If anything happens to Mum, I'll never forgive myself for neglecting her,' she whispered brokenly.

'You haven't neglected her. Even the most dutiful daughter is entitled to a holiday.' Saif crouched down in front of her. 'What's happened?'

'Mum has a chest infection…she's had a few of them but they think she'll have to go into hospital this time,' Tati muttered wretchedly. 'I should've visited her last week, Saif.'

'That wouldn't have prevented her illness,' Saif pointed out shrewdly. 'You will want to return to England as soon as possible. I will make the arrangements.'

While he engaged in phone calls, Tati stayed on the floor, rocking slightly in self-comforting mode as she thought with a shudder about how horribly selfish she had been. She had always placed her mother's needs first…until *Saif* came into her life. And then everything in her world had changed. Saif had turned her world inside out and upside down. Emotions had come surging in a colourful explosion: anger, excitement, attraction, a shocking awakening to all the feelings she had no reason to feel before. And, unforgivably, she had stopped putting her mother first because Saif had turned her head and made her as irresponsible as a teenager.

'I will come with you,' Saif informed her gravely.

'No…no, that's not necessary,' Tati said sharply, reluctant to expose her fragile mother to a stranger, even though she knew that Saif would be kind and respectful. But that protective instinct was hard to combat and, what was more, she didn't want the temptation of Saif being with her in England when she needed to focus solely on her mother.

'I think it is necessary when you will need my support,' Saif overruled.

'If I hadn't been forced to stay abroad, I would never have been away from her for so long,' Tati argued, knowing she was making a veiled and unjust accusation but wanting to punish him as much as she wanted to punish herself. 'Mum's had these infections before. I don't want anyone with me. She gets upset if she sees a strange face, particularly male ones. I don't need you.'

Tati watched his lean, darkly handsome face freeze in receipt of that ungenerous response and her conscience smote her. She didn't need him, couldn't afford to need him, had to persuade herself that she didn't *need* Saif in any corner of her world. Why was it that only at the moment she realised that she *did* crave his support she grasped why it would be even more foolish to rely on him?

Because they weren't a *real* couple or a *real* husband and wife where such troubles as family illness were shared. They were friends with benefits at most, casual lovers at the least and in that type of relationship people didn't get involved in the commitment of deeper problems. And she couldn't afford to forget that because very soon, perhaps sooner than she even believed, she and Saif would be separating, their intimacy at an end. That was what her future held and wanting anything more was nonsensical and unrealistic...

CHAPTER EIGHT

'GO ON,' URGED PAULINE, Mariana Hamilton's cousin, as Tati hovered at the foot of the hospital bed, torn by indecision. 'Your mum's sleeping peacefully. This is the time to go and take care of other things.'

Tati thanked the older woman warmly. In recent days, she had been very grateful for Pauline's unflagging support and affection for her parent. Her mother's chest infection had exacerbated, and she was still in hospital and upsettingly weak. The medical staff seemed to doubt that her mother *could* recover, which had made Tati afraid to abandon her vigil because she didn't want her mother to slip away without her. Lack of sleep had drained her complexion and etched shadows below her eyes.

She had phoned her uncle to update him on her mother's condition but his lack of interest in his sister's state of health had been unhidden. She had explained that she would be calling to collect her possessions and had asked after Ana, relieved but a little surprised to learn that her cousin was currently back at home. If that was true, why on earth hadn't Ana responded to her texts? Tati suppressed her disquiet, which was, after all, only one of several worries haunting her and giving her sleepless nights.

Having initially assured Saif that she would only be away a week, she had now been absent for almost three. He had suggested that he join her, had offered his assistance, had, in short, done everything a committed partner could be expected to do in such circumstances, but Tati had held him at arm's length. After all, their marriage was only temporary, and he had no obligation towards her mother. But at heart, Tati had a far stronger and more personal reason for avoiding Saif: the pregnancy test awaiting her in her hotel bathroom. If her worst fears were proved to have a solid basis in fact, she didn't know what she would do or even how she would face telling him.

Was sheer cowardice the reason that the test had sat unopened for a week? She was ashamed of her lack of backbone but at the same time she was dealing with the awful awareness that her mother's life was slowly and inexorably draining away. For the moment that was sufficient to cope with.

As she settled into the limousine that Saif had insisted she utilise, she nervously fingered the emerald on the chain that hung beneath her silk shirt. It had become something of a talisman through the dark days of stress and loneliness. She missed him *so* much. Her breath caught in her throat as she stifled an angry sob because she was so furious with herself for failing to keep her emotions under control.

When had she begun caring about Saif, needing him, wanting him around? Those feelings had crept up on her without her noticing in Paris and, now she was deprived of him, those longings and the sense of loss inflicted by his absence had only grown stronger.

She had been in England for only a couple of days when she'd registered that her period was very late. At first, she had blamed that on stress. Eventually, she had acknowledged that the smell of certain foods made her tummy roll and that the coffee she usually enjoyed now tasted bitter. Her breasts were tender and bouts of nausea troubled her at odd times of the day. The fear that she could be pregnant had made her very anxious, but it had still taken time for her to muster the courage to buy a pregnancy test. She would do the test once she got back to the hotel, she told herself ruefully. No more putting it off!

Pulling up outside her uncle and aunt's home, Fosters Manor, Tati was enormously conscious that she was making a swanky arrival in a limo accompanied by a carload of diligent security men. As she climbed out, she straightened the light jacket she wore teamed with neat-fitting cigarette pants, a silk top and high heels. Yes, her life and her appearance had certainly changed, she reflected ruefully, heading for the front entrance rather than the rear one that she had once used.

'You can wait for me in the car,' she told the men standing behind her. 'I'll be an hour at most.'

Not one of them moved an inch into retreat, she noted without surprise. They all became uniformly deaf when her requests contravened Saif's instructions, which seemed to encompass keeping her in physical view at all times. Her aunt answered the doorbell wearing a sour expression.

'It won't take me long to pack up,' she assured the older woman quietly.

'It's been done for you,' Elizabeth Hamilton asserted, indicating the dustbin bags messily littering a corner of the dusty hall.

'Oh, thanks,' Tati said stiffly, forcing a fake polite smile and advancing on the collection, leafing through the pile for the only items of value in her care. 'Mum's jewellery box doesn't seem to be here. It's probably still sitting on the dressing table,' she remarked.

Elizabeth's face froze. 'What would you want with that old thing?'

'I want it because it's Mum's. I'll go and fetch it,' Tati said decisively, directing her companions towards the pathetic collection of bags and asking them to put them in the car.

As she started upstairs, her aunt said thinly, 'That box contained some of Granny Milly's pieces.'

'Yes, and they belong to my mother,' Tati retorted crisply. 'They were given to her by *her* mother.'

'I think you and my sister have done well enough out of this family,' Rupert Hamilton informed her from a doorway, his big bluff form spread in an aggressive stance. 'The jewellery should stay with us where it belongs.'

'No,' Tati argued, lifting her chin. 'Any dues my mother or I owed were paid in full in Alharia.'

'Call off your watchdogs!' her uncle instructed with a scowl as two of her protection team followed her upstairs.

Ignoring him, Tati continued up another two flights to her small bedroom. It wasn't quite in the attic, but it was close enough and in bygone days it *had* been a maid's room. It was a relief to see her mother's jewellery box on the dressing table but when she opened it, she found that it contained only the inexpensive costume pieces. A pearl pendant and earrings and a rather distinctive diamond swan brooch were missing. She tucked the box under her arm, wondering what to do next, reluctant to stage a showdown with her relatives that there would be no coming back from, wondering what Saif would advise because he had a cool head.

'Well, well, well, you're looking…*different*.' Ana selected the word with a sneering curl of her lip as she leant against the landing wall. 'Very fancy.'

'Ana!' Tati responded in cheerful relief at seeing

her cousin again. 'Why haven't you called me or answered my texts? Did you change your number?'

'Why would I call you when you stole my bridegroom?' Ana asked with wide eyes, shattering Tati with that absurd question.

'What happened with George?' Tati asked gently.

Ana contorted her lovely face into a grimace. 'He only proposed to stop me marrying someone else. He wasn't willing to set a wedding date once I was home again.'

'I'm so sorry,' Tati said truthfully.

'Oh, I'm sure you're not… How could you be?' Ana demanded thinly, her voice a rising crescendo of complaint. 'My departure worked out *very* well for you. You married a billionaire and now travel around in a flippin' limousine with bodyguards! You robbed me of what should have been mine!'

Mindful of the presence of the protection team, Tati winced. 'Let's talk downstairs in private,' she suggested.

'I don't want to talk about it,' Ana told her stridently. 'I want you to step aside, agree to a divorce and give me back the future you stole from me!'

Tati frowned at that preposterous suggestion. Ana talked as if Saif had no will of his own and as though Tati had entered the marriage freely, which she had not. 'It's not that simple, Ana,' she responded quietly.

'It can be as simple as you're willing to make it. I mean, the Prince would be getting a far superior bride in me. I'm a beauty, classy and educated, the perfect fit for a royal role, which you are not!' her cousin proclaimed as she stomped down the stairs in Tati's wake. 'And I saw a picture of him in the papers.'

Tati faltered. 'A picture?'

'Yes…a photo of you with *him* in Paris,' Ana told her bitterly. 'He's wasted on you. He's absolutely gorgeous! I'd never have walked away had I seen him first!'

'That's…unfortunate,' Tati remarked, although she was terribly tempted to laugh out loud. If George had gone ahead and kept his promise to marry her cousin, Ana would have abandoned all thought of Saif, but because George had disappointed her Ana was looking back with regret to what might have been.

'It's more than unfortunate, Tati!' Ana almost spat at her in her resentment. 'It's wrong and unforgivable that you, a member of my own family, should have taken this opportunity from me!'

'Ana…' Tati's voice was reduced to a discreet whisper. 'I married him in your place because your father threatened to stop paying for my mother's care home. Let's please stick to the facts.'

It amazed Tati how calm and unintimidated she now felt in the face of her relatives' animosity. She rather suspected that Saif's attention and support had contributed to the stronger backbone she had developed.

Her cousin gave her a stubborn, stony appraisal and went on downstairs ahead of her. Tati reached the hall with relief, eager to be gone. The box tucked below her arm, however, slid out of her precarious hold and fell on the rug. In that instant as she stooped down to retrieve it, the emerald round her neck swung out from beneath her shirt into view and glittered in the light.

'Good grief!' Ana exclaimed, reaching forward and almost strangling Tati in her eagerness as she yanked her closer to get a better look at the jewel. 'Is that real? A real emerald *that* size? And there're diamonds all around it!'

Tati's fingers closed over the chain to stop it biting into her neck. 'That's enough, Ana…'

One of her bodyguards stepped forward. 'Let the Princess go before you hurt her,' he told Ana curtly.

Disconcerted, Ana dropped the emerald and took a step back. 'I *feel* like hurting her!' she snapped back in a sudden burst of spite.

'You don't mean that,' Tati said gently, but she was taken aback when her cousin slanted her a look of open resentment.

Sadly, she knew and understood Ana well enough to comprehend her feelings. Ana envied what she saw as Tati's good fortune and believed that Tati had moved up in the world at her expense. She took no heed of the reality that Tati had not wanted to marry Saif in her cousin's place. She chose to forget that she had not been willing to marry Saif sight unseen and had opted to turn her back on the marriage. All she saw now was how handsome Saif was, and the designer garments and the valuable, opulent emerald that Tati wore that had ignited Ana's avaricious streak. Ana felt cheated even though she had chosen to walk away.

Unexpected and unwelcome tears stung Tati's eyes as she climbed back into the limousine to be driven back to the hotel. She had always been very fond of her cousin and until now she had had a much warmer relationship with Ana than she had ever had with her uncle and aunt. Rupert Hamilton and his wife had looked at their niece as though they hated her too and she couldn't understand why.

Did she remind her uncle so strongly of her mother? What had she ever done to them to deserve such treatment? Hadn't she done them a favour by marrying Saif when their daughter ran away? Hadn't that been what they wanted her to do? And now that her mother was so ill, couldn't her brother have some compassion and forgive and forget the petty resentments he had cherished throughout his life?

As for her mother's missing jewellery, what was she planning to do about that? It had to be returned. Those were family keepsakes she valued. She would have to phone her uncle and speak to him once tempers had hopefully settled.

Entering the luxury suite that had been put at her disposal, thanks to Saif, who saw no reason why his wife should sleep in one single room when she could have a giant lounge and two bedrooms all to herself, she went into the bathroom to freshen up and the first thing she saw was that wretched pregnancy test. Gritting her teeth, she picked it up, wondering why she was hesitating when she had to find out one way or another. After all, she might be worrying about nothing!

Ten minutes later she sat staring at the result, her tummy flipping at the confirmation she had received. She had told Saif she was on the pill and, whether she liked it or not, that had been a lie when she had accidentally left her contraceptive supply behind in England. After the test she had planned to acquire a fresh prescription with which to return to Alharia, but that precaution would be wasted when she had already conceived.

For an instant her despondency lifted and a sense of wonder filled her while she allowed herself to imagine a little boy or girl, who would be a mix of her genes and the genes of the man she loved. And she *did* love him, she thought ruefully. There was little point telling herself that it was an infatuation that would soon dissipate when she had fallen head over heels for Saif in Paris. Sizzling chemistry had first knocked her off her safe, sensible perch and scrambled her wits, but the connection had turned into a much deeper attachment on her side. They had shared a magical few weeks, and all her common sense had melted away in the face of Saif's charismatic appeal. But there would be nothing magical about his reaction to the latest development, she reflected unhappily. Saif had warned her that a pregnancy would be an undesirable consequence, a *complication*. She shivered at the memory as she changed to return to the hospital.

And how would he feel about having a child with a woman who wasn't a permanent part of his life? With his own history of maternal abandonment, might it not make his reaction even more emotive?

That evening, her mother passed away without ever regaining consciousness. Tati had fully believed that she was prepared, but when it happened shock flooded her. As she left the hospital again, Pauline gave her a consoling hug before heading for the exit that lay closest to her home. When Tati turned away again in search of the limousine, she saw Saif striding towards her across the car park. Her steps quickened. Her gut reaction was to run to him. She had never been more grateful in her life to see anyone. She was at her lowest ebb and Saif had arrived. Without even thinking about it, she flung herself at him.

'You should've let me join you sooner,' Saif

scolded, holding her fast, so strong, so reliable, so reassuring.

A stifled sob rattling in her throat, she allowed him to tuck her into the car drawing up. 'I didn't ask you to come and yet here you are.'

'I've been keeping in touch with the hospital, following the situation. I'm so sorry, Tatiana,' he breathed, his deep dark drawl hoarse with sympathy. 'I would have flown over last week, but you were insistent on doing this alone.'

'I've always done stuff like this alone...apart from Pauline, and she only moved here after her husband died, and began visiting Mum a couple of years ago,' she muttered shakily. 'I'm so tired, you wouldn't believe how tired I am.'

'It's anxiety and exhaustion. And you have been skipping meals, which won't have helped,' Saif remarked with disapproval.

'Sometimes I haven't been hungry... How do you know that?' And then comprehension set in. 'The protection team...my goodness, they're like a little flock of spies, aren't they?'

'It is their job to look after your well-being in my absence. I also believe you visited your aunt and uncle today and that there was an unpleasant scene,' Saif breathed in a driven undertone. 'I did ask you to stay away from them.'

'Later, Saif,' she sighed, her face buried in a broad shoulder as he kept his arm round her and she drank in the warm familiar scent of him. 'We can talk about it later.'

Afterwards, Tati barely remembered returning to the hotel. She did recall having a meal set in front of her and Saif encouraging her to eat. She had the vaguest recollection of her determination to have a bath and although she recalled getting into the warm scented water, she did not recall getting out of it again. She wakened alone in the bed and, in reliving the day's sad events, suddenly felt a fierce need for Saif's presence. She slid out of bed and padded out to the lounge where he was working on his laptop while watching the business news.

'Sorry, I just collapsed, didn't I?' She sighed. 'Now I have arrangements to make.'

'Those arrangements are being dealt with by my staff. The care home manager permitted me access to your mother's wishes with regard to her interment. I believe she wrote her instructions before she even entered the home,' Saif told her, striving not to stare at her in the fine cotton top and shorts he had put her in after he had lifted her fast asleep out of the bath.

Days of watching her mother's slow decline had marked her, bringing a new fragility to her delicately boned face and shadowing her eyes but in no way detracting from her luminous beauty. He shifted where he stood, uncomfortably aroused. He had pretty much stayed in that condition since he'd found her asleep in the bath and, in the circumstances of her grief, he was anything but proud of his susceptibility.

The weeks without her had been long and empty. For the first time, small foolish things had annoyed him: stodgy courtiers, petty squabbles, long boring meetings. Usually he took such issues in his stride as part and parcel of his life as his father's representative, but recently his temper had taken on a hair-trigger sensitivity and he had had to watch his tongue. His father's adviser, Dalil Khouri, had infuriated Saif by drawing the Emir's attention to a photograph in the newspapers of that stupid kiss in Paris, using it as ammunition in his eagerness to show Tatiana to be an unsuitable wife, who lacked the formality and restraint Dalil believed a royal wife should have. Of course, Dalil had only been trying to do Saif a favour by encouraging his father's disapproval in the belief that it would enable Saif to request a divorce sooner. It had been unexpectedly funny, however, when the Emir startled them all by chuckling and telling his son that he had hoped he would have fun in Paris and, by the looks of it, he *had*.

Tatiana was grieving for her lost parent in a way he himself had never had the chance to do, for how could he have grieved for a woman he had never met, a woman who had walked away while he was still a babe in arms? For that reason he was keen to give his wife all the support he could during so testing a time.

'Thanks,' Tati said in a wobbly voice. 'You know, I thought I was prepared for this.'

Saif set down the laptop and rose fluidly upright, very tall and dark and breathtakingly handsome in the open-necked black shirt and jeans he now wore. Her heart skipped a beat, her mouth ran dry as she thought of what she was hiding from him and instinct almost made her hand slide protectively across her still-flat stomach. She resisted the urge while wondering if she ought to be afraid.

How big a complication would her pregnancy prove to be? Would he ask her to consider a termination? Although he had no hope of persuading her into that choice, she conceded ruefully. She wanted her child even if it hadn't been planned, even if that was an inconvenient preference. But at the same time, she also wanted her child to have a father, because she hadn't had one of her own and knew how much that could hurt.

She would tell him about the baby once they had returned to Alharia, she decided, when life had calmed again, when she had recovered from the first vicious onslaught of loss and felt more able to cope with the stress.

'Tell me about your visit to your relatives,' Saif prompted.

Tati winced. 'Actually, I wanted your advice about something,' she admitted, and she told him about her mother's jewellery. 'She was given the pearls on her eighteenth birthday and the diamond brooch on her twenty-first and I want them back because they have great sentimental worth and Mum loved them.'

'Leave the matter with me. I will handle it,' Saif assured her.

Tati breathed in deep. 'I didn't…er…want to get a solicitor or anything involved,' she warned him. 'When all is said and done, they are still my family.'

'Even when a family member assaults you?'

Tati paled. 'It *wasn't* an assault! The emerald simply attracted Ana's attention and she wanted a closer look at it.'

'If you say so,' Saif sliced in, even white teeth flashing against his bronzed skin, his spectacular green eyes unimpressed by that plea and cool as ice. 'But I say that you are not safe in that house and that you will not be returning there unless I am with you.'

And she thought that that protective instinct of his was one very good reason why she had fallen in love with him. After all, nobody had ever tried to protect Tati before. When she had been oversensitive as a child her mother had simply talked to her about the need to grow a tougher skin. At school she had been bullied and the bullying had been even worse in her uncle's house. Saif, however, stepped right in to help and protect on instinct. And that drew her, of course, it did, particularly when she was feeling vulnerable and raw. Yet she was equally aware that normally she cherished the concept of independence and was keen to make her own decisions, options that her mother's illness had long denied her.

Saif extended a hand to her and drew her down on a sofa beside him. 'Now share your happiest memories with your mother with me...it will help you to keep them alive and turn your thoughts in a better direction. I have no memories whatsoever of my mother, so make the most of what you have left.'

Tears burned and brimmed in her eyes and she blinked them away, digging deep for self-discipline before speaking.

In the early hours, she climbed into bed, lighter of heart and having talked herself hoarse. Saif emerged from the en-suite bathroom still towelling himself dry, black hair ruffled, green eyes very bright against his bronzed skin. Her gaze strayed down the long length of his body, grazing wide shoulders, corrugated abs, a taut, flat stomach, and turbulent warmth tugged at the heart of her, shocking her with its urgency. She lay down and closed her eyes.

'My life felt dull without you around,' Saif breathed in a driven undertone.

Heartened by that admission, Tati slid her hand across the divide between them and closed it over his. 'You can't expect ordinary routine to live up to three sunny weeks in Paris,' she teased.

'It's not a matter of comparisons. You're not always going to be a part of my life and I must adjust to that,' Saif pronounced very seriously.

For a split second it was as though he had plunged a knife into her heart with that reminder and then her natural spirit rallied. 'But I'm here right now,' she pointed out daringly.

'Yes, you are,' Saif conceded huskily as he tugged her closer. 'And nobody has the ability to foretell the future.'

'That's right,' she agreed, frustrated when he made no further move.

'You must be tired.'

'Not since I slept the evening away,' Tati told him, leaning over him and then slowly, gently bringing her lips down to his, because there was a great driving need in her to reconnect again and to make the most of every moment left with him.

Saif lifted a hand and framed her flushed face. 'I assumed touching you would be inappropriate. I didn't want to get it wrong.'

'I want to forget the last three weeks,' she confessed. 'I don't want to think.'

He circled her lips with his and hauled her down to him without any further ceremony, tasting her soft lips with a scorchingly hungry kiss. While he kissed her, he dealt with removing her pyjamas with ruthless expertise. He rolled her under him, parting her legs and sliding his lean hips between her thighs. Her entire body stimulated, she quivered, momentarily mindless with desire, her fingers curling convulsively into his smooth back as he drove into her in one masterful stroke. Jolt after jolt of pure pleasure coursed through her as the excitement mounted. All the tension that had held her taut was now locked in her pelvis and when the exhilaration peaked and she almost passed out from the intensity of her climax, she held fast to him in the aftermath, lost in the blissful wash of relaxation.

'I almost forgot to use a condom.' Saif laughed as he rolled back, carrying her with him. 'You get me so worked up I can still be careless.'

And that was the instant that she should have spoken up. She recognised it as the moment immediately and froze, the truth of her condition clawing at her conscience, but her lips remained stubbornly sealed. Her confession might well lead to an angry confrontation and more distress and worry and right then she couldn't face it.

Reality reminded her that she had entered an intimate relationship in which conception was forbidden from the outset. She had acted without due consideration or concern because the risk of pregnancy had not crossed her mind. Saif might joke that she made him careless, but *she* was the one who had been thoughtless and had chosen not to speak up at the time her oversight occurred. She had conserved her pride rather than lose face and she had simply hoped for the best.

And the price of that silence had now truly come home to roost and there would be no escaping the fallout. Saif would hate that she hadn't warned him. He would hate how long it had taken for her to come clean and own up. He would hate the whole situation and maybe by the end of it he would hate her as well…

CHAPTER NINE

TATI STUDIED SAIF over breakfast in the sun-dappled courtyard, around which their wing of the old palace was built. Her surroundings were beautiful, and she was very much at peace there. Colourful mosaic tiles covered the ground around the softly playing fountain that kept the air fresh and cool. Palm trees and mature shrubs provided shade from the hot sun above while a riot of exotic flowers tumbled round the edges of the dining area.

Saif was checking the business news on a tablet, black hair flopping over his brow, lustrous black lashes shading his spectacular eyes.

'I need to talk to you this evening,' she mustered the courage to announce, because if she mentioned that necessity in advance she couldn't then weaken and back out of it again.

'What about?' Saif sent her an enquiring glance from glittering light green eyes that riveted her where she sat and sent entire flocks of butterflies fluttering inside her.

'Just something important that we need to discuss,' Tati extended uneasily.

Saif did not like to be kept in suspense. 'What's wrong with right now?'

Like the answer to a prayer, Dalil Khouri appeared in the doorway opposite, bowing his head deferentially as he greeted them and addressed Saif. Saif rose with a determined smile to greet the older man. His unfailing courtesy in the face of the constant demands on his time never failed to impress Tati. He was very tolerant. She hoped he brought that tolerance to the fore when she admitted that she was carrying his baby. But she needed the rest of the day to work out the right words with which to frame that admission and that was why Dalil's interruption had been timely.

Tati had learned that the royal palace was always a frantically busy place. Everyone had a role and a schedule, even her. She was currently attending language classes every morning while also enjoying the benefits of a tutor employed to give her a crash course on Alharia's history and culture.

'You cannot be left so ignorant of our country that you will be embarrassed,' Saif had told her. 'People ask questions at the events we attend. I hope you won't object to being effectively sent back to school.'

And she had merely chuckled and shaken her head while wondering what the point of such lessons was intended to be when she wasn't likely to be Saif's wife for longer than a year at most. But at a dinner she had attended with him at an embassy earlier that week, she had been grateful for the ability to join in on a discussion relating to Alharia's current dealings with one of its neighbours.

Only two weeks had passed since her mother's funeral. Her uncle and aunt had not put in an appearance, which had very much shocked Saif's sense of propriety. That evening while she was packing, Saif had gone out for a couple of hours and when he had reappeared he had handed her two worn jewellery boxes that were familiar to her. In wonder she had studied the pearl set and the swan brooch that had belonged to her late mother and she had looked at Saif and asked, 'How on earth did you manage to get hold of them?'

'I simply told your uncle that your mother's possessions should be returned to you. He apologised and blamed your aunt for taking the items. He said she was like a magpie with jewels. I believe that your relatives were so used to taking advantage of your good nature that they assumed they could get away with their behaviour… Now they know different,' he had completed with satisfaction.

'Thank you… Thank you so much,' Tati had told him, relieved that he had understood how precious her mother's former possessions now were to her.

Back then, on the brink of a return to Alharia, it hadn't occurred to her that she might struggle to find the optimum moment in which to tell Saif that she was pregnant. Unfortunately, work had engulfed him in long working hours when they had first come back, and he had been very much preoccupied. They were only ever reliably alone in bed, but she had shrunk from destroying those brief moments of trust and relaxation with a shock announcement. Only now, after almost two weeks of procrastination, was it finally dawning on her that there *was* no right moment for such a revelation. As if the timing were likely to influence his attitude!

Thoroughly exasperated by her apprehensions, Tati thrust away her plate impatiently and leapt up, stepping away from her chair. Her head swam sickly and she tried to grab the stone table as everything swam out of focus, but the darkness rushed in on her and she folded down onto the ground in a heap.

She surfaced groggily to discover that she was lying on her bed with an older man gazing down at her. 'I'm Dr Abaza, Your Highness, the Emir's personal physician. May I have your permission to examine you?'

'Is that necessary?'

'It's necessary,' Saif asserted, stepping forward out of the shadows to make her aware of his presence. 'I would prefer you to have an examination. You passed out. It's possible that you have caught an illness.'

Registering the gravity stamped on his lean, dark

features, Tati subsided, quietly responding to the doctor's polite questions and realising too late the direction in which those questions were travelling. Bearing in mind that she was on the very brink of telling Saif the truth, she could not lie, and as she answered she could not work up the courage to look at him. Dr Abaza completed a brief physical examination and smiled at her. 'I will carry out a test later to be sure, but I am almost certain that you are pregnant. Certain distinct signs characterise a first pregnancy. Low blood pressure most probably caused you to faint. It is a common issue in the first trimester but, naturally, you must guard against it lest you injure yourself in a fall.'

The silence seemed to stretch into every corner of the room and back again and Tati could hardly bring herself to draw breath. She heard Saif thank the doctor. Ice trickled through her veins as he closed the door again.

'How long have you known?' The simplicity of that first question startled Tati.

'I…I—'

'When the doctor told you, it was obvious that you were not surprised. You were already aware of your condition,' Saif conjectured with disturbing discernment. 'For how long have you known?'

'Well, I suspected weeks ago but I sort of…sort of chose to ignore my suspicions.'

'You *ignored*?' Saif emphasised in open disbelief.

'I didn't think it was very likely and I was coping with Mum's illness. I didn't do a test until just before you arrived in England,' she recited breathlessly as she dug in her elbows and sat up.

'But that was over two weeks ago!' Saif exclaimed.

'I was planning to tell you this evening.'

'You should have told me the instant you had grounds for concern,' Saif grated, striding away from her only to swing back, green eyes iridescently bright with anger in his lean bronzed face. 'You have been less than honest with me.'

In receipt of that condemnation, Tati lost colour and slid her legs off the side of the bed. At least he hadn't outright labelled her a liar, she thought ruefully. But she also wondered if his own mother's desertion had made him so wary of women and pregnancy that he expected the very worst of her.

Saif made a commanding staying motion with one hand. 'Don't stand up until you're quite sure that you're not dizzy.'

'Telling you sooner than this that I was pregnant wouldn't have changed anything.' Tati argued her case tautly, still perched on the side of the bed.

'Regrettably, nothing you have yet shared tells me *how* this happened,' Saif framed grimly. 'I believed we had taken every possible precaution.'

'I know that I told you it was safe that first night in Paris. I *was* on the pill, but then I had to pack in a hurry to fly to Alharia for the wedding and I forgot to bring the pills with me. So, I wasn't *lying* when I said there wasn't a risk… I just hadn't thought the situation through properly,' she explained uncomfortably. 'It was only afterwards that I realised I'd left the pills behind in England and that I'd already been off them a couple of days before we…er…got together… and that that was dangerous. It was a genuine oversight, but just then it didn't seem like much of a risk.'

'How did unprotected sex fail to strike you as a risk?' Saif shot at her with raw incredulity.

Tati reddened at his tone and then she shrugged. 'It was only the once and I assumed I would still be semi-protected by the pills I had already taken that month. You were very careful after that, so I thought we would be all right. I didn't see any reason to worry you when there was probably going to be nothing to worry about.'

'You should have told me. I had a right to know,' Saif breathed in a driven undertone as he paced in front of the doors that led out to a balcony.

'Yes, but the only option at that point would have been me taking a morning-after pill and I didn't feel comfortable with that option,' Tati admitted bluntly.

'I would not have suggested that, but I dislike the fact that you chose to keep me in the dark when I am *equally* affected by this development!' Saif shot back at her crushingly.

It was a fair point and she didn't argue. 'Well, at

least you know now,' she pointed out, feeling forced into the role of Job's comforter.

'I should think that half the palace is now aware of Dr Abaza's diagnosis!' Saif retorted drily. 'He will have reported straight back to my father and I would imagine others will have overheard sufficient to comprehend.'

'For goodness' sake…' Tati groaned in embarrassment.

'Why? It's not as though it is something that you could keep a secret for much longer.' Saif subjected her to a long intense appraisal. 'You're carrying my child. That is very big news in Alharia so we could not hope to keep it to ourselves. I very much doubt that you currently appreciate how much this development will impact our situation, which is naturally why I tried to ensure that it didn't occur.'

Tati stood up and lifted her head high, rumpled blond hair rippling round her shoulders, blue eyes mutinous. 'Oh, do stop talking in that deadly tone, as though it's the end of the world. It's a baby…and I love babies! I mean, we didn't plan this, and I know you like to plan stuff in advance, but how much difference can one little baby make to our *situation*, as you call it?'

Saif dealt her a bleak appraisal. 'A huge difference. I would never have chosen to conceive a child in a marriage that is not intended to last. I *know* what that situation is like from my own childhood. It is unfair to our child and will likely affect his or her emotional well-being and sense of security.'

'Don't talk to me as though I'm stupid, Saif,' Tati countered angrily, her eyes flaring with temper. 'Neither of us planned this. Both of us tried to be careful. Yes, I agree it's *not* perfect, but neither of us had perfect when it came to parents and *we* survived!'

'It's clear to me that you have still not thought through the ramifications of this development and the effect it will have on *your* freedom,' Saif grated, raking lean brown fingers through his black hair in a gesture of unconcealed frustration. 'My mother didn't want this sort of life in Alharia and she walked away from it. How will you be any different? The main point I would make is that although you grew up without a father and I grew up without a mother, neither of us was torn between two opposing households and cultures.'

'Parents do successfully work together to raise children after a divorce,' Tati protested. 'We're not enemies. We're both rational, reasonable people.'

'If you give birth to a boy he will be an heir to the Alharian throne and he will have to spend the majority of his time in *this* country, which will naturally have an influence on where you choose to live,' Saif spelt out.

'Why would he have to spend the majority of his time here?' Tati demanded with a frown.

'How else could he prepare for his future role? He

must grow up amongst our people, with the language
and the culture. His education and future training
would be of the utmost importance and could not
be achieved if his main home were to be in another
country. And if you have a girl, she may well be the
next ruler because I have every intention of chang-
ing the constitution when I ascend the throne. It is
what our people want and expect in these days of
equality,' Saif completed, his darkly handsome features troubled and taut. 'I would not want to see my
child, girl or boy, only occasionally or for visits. That
would bother me.'

Tati was tense. 'It would bother me as well. So,
you're saying that to share a child I would have to
make a home for myself in Alharia.'

'Yes. Becoming parents will make a clean break
impossible,' Saif delivered heavily. 'I appreciate how
much that would detract from your independence.'

Tati was almost paralysed by the pain of hearing Saif refer to the option of 'a clean break.' In that
scenario, after a divorce he would never have had to
see her again and obviously that would have been
his preference. Yet the same concept devastated her
even as she finally grasped the obvious truth that
the birth of a child would entangle their lives for a
long time and that, self-evidently by his tone, was
not what Saif wanted. He didn't *want* to share a child
with an ex who lived elsewhere. How could she hold
such honesty against him? But why did he have to

be such a pessimist about the future? Why couldn't he make the best of things as she was striving to do?

'Your attitude annoys me,' Tati told him honestly. 'I tend to believe that the mixing of two cultures and lifestyles is more likely to enrich our child.'

'In an ideal world,' Saif slotted in grimly. 'But we don't live in one. If this *were* an ideal world, I would be able to openly acknowledge to my father that I have a close relationship with my half-brother, Angelino Diamandis.'

'You have a brother?' Tati exclaimed in complete surprise, disconcerted by that sudden revelation from a man who could, at the very least, be described as reticent.

'He is two years younger than I, born from my mother's second marriage. I sought him out years ago, but I think initially I wanted to meet him to see what he had that I didn't because my mother stuck around to raise him,' he pointed out curtly, the darkening of his bright eyes the proof of how emotive that topic was for him. 'Instead I discovered that my half-brother had enjoyed little more mothering than I had and I was surprised at the depth of the bond that developed between us. That relationship, however, had to remain a secret because I did not want to upset my father. He was devastated by my mother's desertion and the wound never really healed because after her second marriage she was rarely out of the newspapers. She was a great beauty and she revelled in publicity,' Saif explained ruefully. 'Children born across the divide of divorce are often placed in difficult positions out of loyalty to their respective parents. Step-families are created and other children follow. The experience may strengthen some, but it injures others.'

'That relative of yours who owns the house in Paris. Is that your brother?' Tati prompted with sudden comprehension.

'Yes, that house belongs to Angel. He also attended my wedding incognito and I got to spend some time with him before he had to leave again,' Saif told her. 'I value my relationship with my younger brother although it shames me to keep it a secret from my father. However, I cannot mention my mother or her second family to him without causing him great distress, which I obviously don't want to do when his health is poor.'

'He must really have loved her to still be so sensitive… Or is he just bitter?' Tati questioned with open curiosity.

'No, she was truly the love of my father's life, but the marriage was always destined to fail,' Saif opined fatalistically. 'She was too young and worldly, and he was too old and traditional. When you consider the very public social whirl she embarked on after deserting her husband and son in Alharia and her complete lack of regret for what she had done, you realise that they were ill-suited from the start.

Whatever else he may be, my father is a most compassionate man. Had she given him the opportunity he would have given her a divorce and there would not have been a huge scandal. But the Emir was not the only one to suffer her loss... I did as well and spent many years wondering why she couldn't have stayed for my benefit.'

'That's very sad,' Tati acknowledged reflectively. 'But not really relevant to us. I'm not planning on deserting anyone, least of all my child, nor am I the sort of person attracted to the idea of publicity.'

'Who can tell what you will be enjoying in a few years' time?' Saif said with sardonic bite, his sheer cynicism infuriating her.

'You are such a pessimist!' Tati exclaimed. 'Do you always expect the very worst of people?'

'I'm a realist, not a pessimist. I would be foolish to ignore the truth that you will be a young and very wealthy divorcee and that inevitably you will remarry, have other children and change from the woman you are now,' Saif breathed, untouched by her criticism.

'I bet that, right now, you are really, *really* regretting that you consummated our marriage!' Tati accused tempestuously.

'My only regret is that I wanted you so much that I went along with that "friends with benefits" idea even though I *knew* from the outset that it was absolute madness!' Saif flung back at her in a raw-edged tone of self-loathing.

Tati froze as though she had been slapped and lost colour. It was clear that Saif could not get onboard with her conviction that they should make the best of her pregnancy. He hadn't planned the conception; he hadn't agreed to it and he seemed unlikely to move on from that position. But it was even worse to be confronted with the truth that he now regretted their relationship in its entirety.

'Madness,' she repeated through taut, dry lips with distaste, feeling totally rejected.

'What else could it be in our circumstances? This relationship of ours is insane and you know it!' Saif condemned harshly. 'Once we had both acknowledged that we didn't want to be married, we should have abstained from sex.'

Tati reddened. 'You weren't a great fan of abstinence either,' she reminded him accusingly.

'I am not solely blaming you,' Saif countered grittily. 'I was also tempted, and I gave way to that temptation, but it is exactly that self-indulgence that has landed us both into this predicament. A divorce is out of the question for the foreseeable future.'

'But why?' Tati prompted in stark disconcertion at that statement.

'It is far too soon for us to separate and I refuse to seek a divorce from a pregnant wife. I should be with you during your pregnancy, offering whatever support I can. I feel equally strongly that for the first crucial years of our child's life we should remain together, trying to be the best parents we can be for our child's benefit,' Saif explained heavily. 'It would be selfish to only consider our own wants and needs. I wouldn't ever want our child to know the pain of not being wanted by a parent.'

His outlook made Tati feel wretched and like the most selfish woman in the world. She stood up to move towards the door, saying, 'I have a language lesson in ten minutes, and I don't want to miss it. We can talk later, and it might help a lot if you could come up with something positive rather than *negative*.'

Saif swore under his breath as she left the room. So fierce was his frustration that he was tempted to punch the wall, but bruises and a loss of temper would not change anything, he reflected with grim resignation. His wife was planning to leave him just as his mother had left his father and her son. Saif, however, was determined not to lose either of them. There was also a very real risk of his losing his child because Tatiana was, he surmised, a great deal more maternal than his mother had been.

In a different scenario he would have been overjoyed at the news that he was to become a father and he was angry at being deprived of that natural response, but it was, sadly, an issue clouded by his own experiences. Being abandoned by his mother soon after birth had hurt and changed his attitude to childbirth and parenthood because he already knew that he could never leave his child as his mother had done.

Yet how could he celebrate the birth of a child in a marriage that was a fake? A marriage that had been deemed over before it even properly began? Tatiana had never given him a fair chance, not one single chance. She had not budged an iota in her attitude since their first day together. She expected and wanted a divorce as her recompense for agreeing to a marriage that she had been blackmailed into accepting. And during the weeks they had been together she had frequently alluded to the prospect of that divorce and was obviously perfectly content with that outcome. And, even more revealing, she had refused Saif's support when her own mother was dying. She had in every possible way treated Saif as though he was superfluous, merely a casual sexual partner in a fling without a future. What she had never done, he thought painfully, was treat him like a friend.

And how much could he blame her for her attitude when he had become her first lover? Tatiana had had a difficult life with little liberty, even less money and few choices, he reminded himself. Furthermore, although she had yet to find it out, she had been ruthlessly used, abused and defrauded by relatives who should have cherished her, most especially after her mother fell ill. Saif frowned, wondering if he should tell her the truth about her grandmother's will and her uncle's wicked greed, but he had withheld what he knew on the basis that the police were in charge of the investigation now and the truth would come out soon enough when arrests were made. Saif had no desire to be the person who broke that bad news and hurt her.

Naturally, that revelation would adversely affect Tatiana because she remained blindly, ridiculously attached to those relatives of hers. From her teenaged years she had depended on them, and they had been all she had once her grandmother died and her mother sank into dementia. She had even excused their greed to Saif by explaining that her uncle had always been hopeless with money and had married an ambitious woman with grand expectations. How would she feel when she appreciated that they had lied and cheated to deprive her of her inheritance and had been busy ever since overspending *her* money as fast as they could?

When that grievous knowledge was unveiled, his bride would be even keener to enjoy the freedom she had never had. The freedom *he* didn't *want* her to have, Saif reflected bitterly. Was it any wonder that he was such a cynic?

Tati struggled through the language lesson with tears burning the backs of her eyes while she fought to relocate some seed of concentration. She struggled to dwell on the positives rather than the negatives of her plight. Saif wanted their baby and was already anxiously considering the potential effect of a divorce on their child. Why didn't he thread her into that problem and realise that if he *stayed* married to her, he wouldn't have to worry about their child's security? Obviously because he didn't *want* to stay married to her, Tati reflected miserably. Why was she set on beating her head up against a brick wall?

And what would it be like to continue living with Saif for another four or five years? Wouldn't that simply make the whole process of breaking up more agonising? It would drag it out and place her under heavier stress. She would always be waiting for the moment when he decided they had stayed together long enough and were in a position to separate. How could a future like that appeal to her?

It would freeze her life and prevent her from moving on. How could she truly move on if she were to be forced to live in Alharia for her son or daughter's sake? The prospect of standing on the sidelines watching Saif with other women, having to share her child with those same women, made her shudder. No, that wouldn't work for her. He would have to come up with a better, more bearable solution. When her mother was ill, she had accepted that being bullied, being forced into a position she didn't want, was a situation she could not escape. But life had changed for her and she herself had changed, she reflected ruefully. Ironically, Saif had made her realise that she was much stronger than she had ever appreciated.

With regard to future arrangements between them
for their child, she was prepared to be reasonable,
but she wasn't a martyr. She would get over him at
some stage, but how was she to achieve that if she
was still forced to live with him?

Saif spent an hour that afternoon listening to his
father wax lyrical about the joys of fatherhood.
Thinking of the disappointments the older man had
suffered in the wife department convinced Saif that
Tatiana had been right to denounce his pessimis-
tic outlook. Somehow, it would all work out, if they
both made an effort, if he controlled the urge to lock
her up and throw away the key, not because he was
a controlling creep, but because, try as he might,
he kept on thinking of the way his mother had just
abandoned ship and run for greener pastures. Might
not Tatiana also choose to bolt if he put too much
pressure on her? She was pregnant and she couldn't
be feeling well when she was fainting, he reasoned
worriedly.

A man famed for his cool, logical approach to
problems, he wondered how it was that in a moment
of crisis he had said and done everything wrong. He
had *told* Tatiana that they would have to stay married for years longer. He had *told* her that she would
have to live in Alharia. How could he have been that
clumsy, domineering and stupid? And he hadn't *once*

mentioned how excited he was about the baby they had conceived.

It was at that point in his ruminations that Dalil Khouri joined Saif to announce that his wife's cousin, Ana Hamilton, had arrived at the airport and intended to visit them. It was normal for an alert to be sent to the palace when a prospective guest arrived, but Saif frowned at that news, questioning why the woman had chosen to fly to Alharia when only months earlier she had run away as fast as she could sooner than marry him. Was it possible that Ana's parents had already been arrested? Could their daughter be here to plead their case? What else could she be doing in Alharia?

Saif appreciated that it was his task to tell his wife what he had learned several weeks earlier because he could not let her meet with her cousin while still in ignorance of his recent discoveries.

'Have her brought to the palace,' he told Dalil. 'But drive her around for a while—take her to see some tourist sight, or something... I don't want my wife to be taken by surprise or upset and I need some time to prepare her for her cousin's arrival.'

'Of course,' Dalil agreed earnestly. 'The Princess must be protected at all costs from anyone who might seek to take advantage of her.'

Tati was enjoying mint tea and a savoury snack in the courtyard when Saif strode down the stairs into the courtyard to join her. He was breathtakingly handsome in an Italian wool-and-silk-mix suit that was exquisitely tailored to his lean, powerful frame. Her wide blue gaze clung to him and then pulled free of him again, her soft mouth tightening as she told herself off for being so susceptible. *That* kind of nonsense, that mooning over him like a silly sentimental schoolgirl, couldn't continue.

'First of all, I bought these for you in Paris, but after your mother fell ill there didn't seem to be a right time to give them to you,' Saif intoned, setting a jewellery box down on the table. 'This seems the appropriate moment to express my happiness about the child you are carrying and present you with this small gift to mark a special occasion.'

'You must've had to dig deep to find that happiness,' Tati opined tartly.

'You took me by surprise, but once the news sank in, I was thrilled,' Saif asserted defiantly in the face of her dubious look. 'Everything changed for me when you told me that you were pregnant. When my mother walked away from me when I was a baby, it made the whole topic very emotional for me. I tried not to dwell on her abandonment. I suppressed the sadness that that awareness inflicted because I believed that that is what a man must do to be a man...'

'Oh, Saif,' she whispered, her body stiffening as she fought the pressing need to go to him, to comfort him, to soothe the hurt he had felt that he had to deny as an adult man. But that was no longer her role, she reasoned. Furthermore, it was becoming ever more clear to her as he talked that Saif was not driven by love to wish to remain married to her for their child's sake but by fear for their child's hurt in the future. She couldn't fault him for that, she decided heavily, but that he should only want to be with her to be a father for their baby pierced her deeply.

Brushing off those emotional responses, Tati flipped open the box on a superb pair of emerald earrings in the same design as the magnificent pendant she wore. 'Wow,' she whispered without being prompted because it was yet another exciting gift that no sane woman could fail to appreciate. 'They're beautiful—'

'Perhaps you could wear them for dinner tonight,' Saif proposed. 'We have a surprise guest joining us.'

'Oh…and who would that be?' Tati gazed at him enquiringly as she twirled the emerald earrings in the sunlight. She put them on with the kind of defiance that denied that there was anything special about the occasion while reminding herself that she ought at least to enjoy the frills while she still could.

'Your cousin, Ana, is about to arrive here,' Saif imparted. 'Of course, you may be grateful for the company of a female friend at the moment.'

Utterly taken aback by the idea of Ana visiting Alharia, Tati stiffened, wondering if it was crazy to suspect that her cousin might be turning up to give Saif a belated opportunity to see what he had missed

out on on his wedding day. When Ana got an idea
into her head, it was hard to shift, although even Tati
was a touch disconcerted by her cousin's lack of embarrassment at visiting the home of the same man
she had refused to marry only weeks earlier. 'Why
would I be grateful?'

Saif breathed in deep. 'Because of the discovery
you have recently made and the complications—'

'I'm not going to share any of that with Ana!' Tati
protested. 'That's *our* business and much too private.'

'I think that is for the best, but before she arrives
there is information about your family which I have
to share with you,' Saif proffered heavily.

Tati became tense, noting the grave expression he
wore. 'What information and about whom?'

'Your uncle and aunt. I'm afraid I genuinely do
not know if your cousin was aware of what's been
going on for the past few years.'

'Going on?' Tati interrupted. 'What do you mean
by "going on"?'

'Three years ago, after your grandmother died,
your uncle and her solicitor worked together to deprive you of your inheritance. Your grandmother
not only set up a trust to cover the cost of your late
mother's care, but she also left the Fosters Manor
estate to you.'

'That's impossible,' Tati broke in afresh. 'I wasn't
left anything! My uncle told me that.'

Saif ignored the interruption. 'You were to inherit the estate when you reached twenty-one, but you were supposed to enjoy the income from it immediately. In effect your uncle was disinherited in your favour. Your uncle had made continual financial demands on your grandparents during their lifetime and your grandmother apparently believed that he had had his fair share before her death. Unfortunately, she appointed both your uncle and the solicitor, Roger Sallow, as executors of the will. The solicitor was corrupt. Your uncle bribed Sallow to remain silent and at the official reading Sallow read an invalid will that had been written years earlier. Your uncle has since made regular very large payments to the solicitor. The size of those payments probably explains his continuing financial troubles because Sallow became increasingly greedy.'

'I can't believe this…' Tati massaged her pounding forehead with her fingers. 'Granny Milly actually chose to leave it all to *me*?' she exclaimed in disbelief. 'How did you find all this out?'

'The day I married you, I asked a private investigation agency to do a report on you,' Saif revealed tautly. 'At that stage, I knew nothing about you and I wanted the facts. The investigator met with an old friend of your grandmother's who had witnessed the will without actually seeing the contents and she chose to share her concerns with him.'

Tati frowned. 'Her concerns?'

'She knew what your grandmother had originally planned and was very surprised when she saw that nothing changed at the manor after her friend's death, but she didn't come forward because she decided that it was none of her business and she didn't wish to offend anyone. She could, of course, have *asked* to see the will, which was on public record, but she didn't know that,' Saif recounted wryly. 'Basically, she is an elderly woman who didn't want to risk getting involved in what she suspected could be a crime.'

Tati parted bloodless lips. 'A crime?'

'You have been defrauded of your rightful inheritance and that is a crime,' Saif pointed out grimly. 'The investigation agency consulted me as soon as they uncovered the irregularities and I told them to find the evidence and put the whole matter in the hands of the police.'

If possible, Tati turned even paler. *'The police?'* she whispered in horror.

'Fraud has been committed, Tatiana,' Saif asserted grimly. 'How else may such wickedness be handled?'

Tati lifted her aching head high and looked back at him with icy blue eyes of condemnation. 'I don't know, Saif. You would need to tell me because, even though this concerns me, *I* wasn't consulted.'

'I imagine the police will seek some sort of statement from you, but they have all the evidence they require for a prosecution.'

Tati nodded, in so much shock that she was barely able to absorb what she had been told. She couldn't quite credit her hearing. She had never liked her uncle, but that he could act so basely and deliberately defraud her, while still treating her like a despised poor relation who was a burden, took her breath away. As for the trust that Saif had mentioned, the trust set up to care for her poor mother's needs, the knowledge that that information had been withheld filled her with nauseated rage on her late parent's behalf. She had been controlled and threatened with lies when all along her uncle had had little choice but to keep on paying those care home bills because stopping payment could have drawn dangerous attention to him.

'*When* did you find all this out?' Tati prompted sickly.

'The first week we were married…well, I didn't know the whole story then, but I was informed that there was every sign that your uncle had committed fraud and that he was being blackmailed by the solicitor for his misdeeds.' Saif studied her anxiously because she was very pale even if she was handling the whole business more quietly than he had somehow expected. 'I didn't want to make allegations against your relatives without adequate proof, which is why I remained silent about my suspicions.'

'And why are you finally telling me now?' Tati enquired stiffly, a glint in her unusually bright gaze, resentment and bitterness and anger all flaring at once inside her.

'Only because your cousin is about to arrive and, if the police have made a move against her father, she could be visiting with a plea that you intervene... although, to be frank, I doubt that you have the power now that the police are involved and have the evidence of his crime.'

'I gather you think that Ana must know about this!' Tati commented stiffly.

'I imagine she does,' Saif said very drily.

'I doubt that very much. Ana is spoiled, selfish and materialistic but she's never been dishonest or cruel. There's no way *she's* involved!' Tati told him with firm emphasis.

'Since you are so fond of her, I can only hope that you are correct.'

'No, my belief is that Ana is visiting to subject you to a charm offensive,' Tati mused, grimacing a little at having to voice that opinion because it mortified her.

'*Me?* A charm offensive?' Saif repeated blankly. 'What are you saying?'

'The man Ana ran away from you to marry let her down and now she has regrets about not marrying you.'

'A little late in the day,' Saif remarked as dry as the desert sand.

'As far as Ana's concerned, I'm only a substitute for her and not a very good one at that,' Tati explained as she rose from her seat. 'You're rich, generous and good-looking. She's probably hoping you'll be willing to consider a swap.'

'A *swap*?' Saif sliced back at her in sheer disbelief.

Tati gave him a long, considering appraisal, ticking all the mental boxes he occupied in her head. It was no wonder she had fallen for him like a ton of bricks when he was gorgeous and capable of immense charm when he wished to utilise it. 'Ana isn't particularly intelligent. But, you know, you would still have done much better with her than with me,' she told him ruefully. 'I doubt that my cousin would ever have become accidentally pregnant.'

'I *am* pleased about our baby,' Saif countered fiercely, displeased by the sarcastic tone of words that hinted that her cousin was welcome to him.

Tati flung up her head, blond strands rippling back from her troubled face, her eyes full of newly learned cynicism. 'So you say...'

CHAPTER TEN

ANA LOOKED STUNNING, her golden hair a silken swathe, her brown eyes beautifully made up, her silky short dress showing off long shapely legs. Initially full of peevish complaints about the 'old boring ruin of a castle' she had been dragged to view by some palace official, she soon switched to a playful smile when she realised that she was being rude. She then embraced Tati without hesitation and pouted in disappointment when Saif excused himself to make a phone call.

'Good grief,' she muttered as the door closed behind Tati's husband. 'Saif's even better looking in the flesh! Those cheekbones, that amazing physique!'

'How's everybody at home?' Tati enquired rather stiffly.

Ana sighed. 'Much the same as usual. Mum's nagging Dad about this autumn cruise she fancies and Dad's saying he doesn't want to miss the start of the shooting season. I'm so sorry I was rude when you came to the manor. Everything just got on top— George, the change in your fortunes…and I missed you.'

'I missed you too.' Warmed by that little speech, Tati searched her cousin's face and was fully satisfied that the blonde had no clue that legal problems could be hovering over her family. *She* herself was still struggling to accept the situation that Saif had outlined. She was outraged that he had kept her out of his enquiries and that only Ana's unexpected arrival had persuaded him to come clean about what was *her* business, rather than his. At heart too she was still reeling in shock at what she had learned while trying not to dwell on what was likely to happen in her marriage in the short term.

Saif didn't love her, and if he wanted her to stay married to him longer it was only because he was keen to protect their child. There was nothing she could do to change that, but she could still act on her own behalf and…walk away. More and more that was what she wanted to do, and she kept on suppressing that thought, reminding herself that her child deserved a father, but still the prospect of escape pulled and tugged seductively at her. Saif had sent her crashing from the heights of happiness down into the depths of despair. If she couldn't have Saif fully and for ever, she didn't want him, and she certainly didn't want some empty, pretend relationship drag-

ging on for years with him, because the pain of that
would kill her by degrees.

'*Oh...my...goodness!*' Ana exclaimed with emphasis, leaning closer to Tati to brush a fingertip against
a dangling emerald earring gleaming like a rainbow
in a shaft of sunlight. 'Now you have earrings worth
a fortune as well!'

'Saif's very generous.'

'Then hand him over,' Ana urged cheerfully, as
if she were asking to borrow something quite incon-
sequential. 'He's the serious type, isn't he? He needs
someone more exciting like me in his life. You could
go back to England and I could—'

Tati's stomach hollowed out. 'I'm pregnant, Ana.
It wouldn't be quite that simple.'

'You mean…' Ana stared at her in open astonishment. 'You mean *you* actually *slept* with him? And
you've conceived?' Ana shook her head slowly and
took a moment to regroup. 'Well, good on you because I don't want kids until I'm well into my thir-
ties.'

Tati wore an impassive expression. 'I think you'll
have to see how Saif feels about that.'

Ana laughed. 'Of course, he'll want me…men
always do!' she carolled with enviable confidence. 'I
could see that he was working hard not to look at me
when I arrived, trying to hide his interest, and now
I understand why. Obviously, if you're pregnant, he
feels he can hardly jump ship.'

Tati wondered if it was true that Saif had been trying to hide his interest. Ana was beautiful, lively and sexy. Of course, he would have noticed, particularly when Tati was pale and quiet because she was barely speaking to him and their relationship was at an all-time low. 'But doesn't it bother you that he's been intimate with me?' she pressed, striving to turn her cousin's thoughts in a more appropriate direction. 'Doesn't that put you off?'

'Oh, not at all. Men aren't that fussy when it comes to a willing woman,' Ana said knowledgeably just as her phone began playing a favourite tune.

Tati knew instantly what the call was about because Ana was no dissembler. Her eyes flew wide and she said sharply, 'You can't be serious! The *police*? I don't believe you!'

While she was talking and becoming more and more distressed, Tati got up and left the room to trek downstairs to Saif's office.

'Ana's just found out that her parents have been arrested…and *no*, she didn't know anything about it. I want to fly back to England with her.'

Brilliant green eyes locked to her flushed face. 'That would be unwise.'

'I don't care whether it's wise or not,' Tati responded truthfully. 'This is a family matter. You interfered and let me find out the hard way, but it's not your decision or your business…it's *mine*.'

'I was trying to protect you. I didn't want to risk

telling you anything false. I don't deal in unsubstantiated stories,' Saif intoned with cool dignity. 'Becoming involved in the fallout from your uncle's actions at this stage could be very challenging for you. You would be in a very awkward position as his victim.'

'I'm not a coward. I can deal with unpleasant things,' Tati told him, lifting her head high.

'If you go to England, I will be accompanying you. We'll fly out in the morning,' Saif announced.

'Even if I don't *want* you to?' Tati snapped angrily.

Saif breathed in deep and slow, his green eyes glittering as bright as the earrings she wore. 'Even then.'

'Well...' Tati stomped back to the door in a temper. 'I'll just ignore you. I'll pretend you're not there getting into business that has nothing to do with you!'

'Everything that relates to you involves me because we're a couple.'

'I wouldn't use that word about us,' Tati said in fierce denial, leaving his office to return to her cousin.

'The police have let them both out on bail and have confiscated their passports like they're *criminals*!' Ana wailed at her incredulously. 'Dad's being charged with fraud and Mum's being charged as an accessory. How on earth could Granny have done this to us? I mean, Dad was the eldest child, everything *should've* gone to him. It's not surprising he went a little crazy and did wrong.'

'Actually, my mother was the eldest by eighteen

months,' Tati chipped in gently as she rubbed her sobbing cousin's spine in a soothing motion.

'But the will that they pretended was still current left the estate to Dad. So, Granny must have changed her mind.' And then Ana sobbed. 'Oh, hell, Tati, how could Dad lie and do such a thing to you when you're part of our family as well? I never dreamt he could sink so low!'

'I think his hatred for my mother...and in her absence, *me*...overwhelmed his judgement. But I shouldn't be discussing this with you, Ana. I'm too close to it. Talk to your friends,' she urged.

'I can't tell *them* about this! When this gets out into the papers everybody will think I'm as guilty as my parents are of robbing you blind!' Ana sobbed. 'Oh, Tati, can't you please stop this happening?'

But as Tati discovered, late the following day when she was interviewed by the police in England and had answered their questions, the prosecution had nothing to do with her. Crimes had been committed and the solicitor was in even more severe trouble than her uncle and was suspected of having suggested the substitution of the outdated will to Rupert Hamilton in the first place. His dealings with his other clients were now under careful scrutiny.

When the official business was complete, Tati felt drained and she climbed into the limo that came to collect her and focused on Saif's lean, darkly handsome features wearily. 'Well, you were right, there's nothing I can do.'

'But why would you *want* to do anything to help your persecutors?' Saif demanded in driven disbelief.

'Not because I forgive them, because I don't,' she said quietly. 'I had a hellish time after Granny passed worrying about my mother's security in the care home. I could never forgive them for that or for treating me like dirt. But I pity Ana because she loves them and she's ashamed and mortified and she had no idea what had been done.'

'Then compensate her in some way if you wish to be generous. You seem to forget that you have become a very wealthy woman with considerable sums at your disposal. What your uncle deprived you of was a mere tithe of what you are now worth,' Saif informed her.

Tati fixed dismayed eyes to him. 'How am I wealthy? You may be, I'm not!'

'When we married, I settled funds on you that would make you wealthy by most people's standards…if not mine,' Saif told her coolly.

Tati clasped her hands together tightly. 'I don't want your money. I'm not being rude or ungrateful, but it's not right for me to be taking money from you when we were never truly married in the first place.'

Saif expelled his breath in a sudden hiss and clamped his even white teeth down on a swear word. *'Truly?'* he derided. 'We had the ceremony. We have shared a bed, made love and conceived a child. How is all that *not* a marriage?'

'The intent was missing. You didn't want to marry me,' Tati reminded him stubbornly.

'Is it enough to say that I would have that intent now and would marry you again, given the chance?' Saif shot at her in a raw undertone.

Tati paled and studied her linked hands, reckoning that he was only saying that because she was pregnant and had to be placated. 'No, it's not. Let's stick to our agreement for the moment.'

'Which agreement? The "friends with benefits" idea seems to have died a death,' Saif breathed curtly. 'The agreement to part within months is impossible as matters stand.'

Tati bowed her head. 'I'm not in the mood to talk about it right now,' she told him shakily, feeling terrifyingly close to a bout of overwrought tears.

She was acting like a shrew and an indecisive one at that, Tati mused guiltily, and yet he had been endlessly kind and supportive. Despite her discouragement, he had escorted her to England and had sent a lawyer to the police station with her when she'd turned down his company. She loved him so much and, even when she was angry with him, that love burned like a torch inside her and made her want to do silly stuff like grab him and hug him just for being there when her life was tough. Nobody prior to Saif had ever stood up for her before. He was so loyal, so caring that he made her love him more than ever, but that only made her feel worse and more of a burden to him.

'Your uncle contacted me this afternoon to request a meeting. He and your aunt have moved out of the manor.'

Tati dealt him a startled look. 'They…they *have*?'

'An obvious first move. It's your house where they treated you like a servant,' Saif pronounced with distaste. 'He will now wish to impress you with his repentance.'

Tati couldn't even picture a repentant version of her pompous relative. 'What did you say?'

'I said it was your decision as to whether or not you would see him,' Saif murmured grimly.

Tati could tell by the hard slant of his wide sensual mouth what *his* decision would have been, but she appreciated that, for once, he hadn't interfered. 'I'll see him at the hotel this evening if it suits.'

For the first time she was asking herself why she had got so very angry with Saif. She had deeply resented the admission that he had known about her uncle's crime before she had, even though she would never ever have found out the truth on her own behalf. She had spent her adult life being pushed around by people with power over her or her mother and she had often been browbeaten into doing what she didn't want to do. Saif had decided that he knew better than her even though the wrongdoers were her relatives, and she knew them best. But there was one crucial difference with Saif, she acknowledged now that she had calmed and taken a step back from shock and anger: Saif did what he did from an engrained need to protect her, not from a desire to belittle or control her, and that made a huge difference.

Tati slanted a glance at his lean, bronzed face, recognising the hard tension bracketing his mouth. 'I'm sorry I've been so unreasonable about all this,' she told him before she could lose her nerve. 'It's such a nasty, sordid business.'

'And I don't want you dealing with this right now,' Saif slotted in honestly, his stunning green eyes enhanced by his dense black lashes.

'It's almost over,' she pointed out. 'And I want to go and see the manor again tomorrow.'

'Why?'

'I spent a lot of my time there when my grandmother was still alive. It was a place of happy memories until Mum fell ill,' she admitted stiffly. 'I refuse to let my last few unhappy years there when my uncle was in charge spoil that for me.'

Saif was prepared to admit that Tatiana had a backbone of steel under that fragile exterior of hers, a quiet dignity, which had very much impressed the lawyer who had been at the police interview with her. He had phoned Saif the instant he'd emerged from it, full of praise for the calm, intelligent manner in which Tatiana had dealt with the situation. But Saif was much less fond of that reference to the house that was hers here in England and her attachment to it. He said nothing, however, convinced that he would strike a wrong note if he commented. He had never been in an equal relationship with a woman before, he reflected with a frown. Perhaps that was why he had erred and dictated rather than discussed.

Her uncle Rupert arrived at eight that evening at their hotel. Tati saw him alone, hardening her heart while he recited his woes and excuses, not to mention his embittered recriminations against the grandmother she had loved. It was always someone else's fault, never his when anything went wrong in Rupert Hamilton's life. When she told him of her decision his mask of discomfiture slipped for a second, and his hatred showed. He argued with her until she lost patience because she could not have cared less what happened to her uncle and aunt or where they went, but their daughter, Ana, was a different issue. If she could protect her cousin she would, and she would not apologise for it. The older man left in a very bad mood.

'I almost intervened when I heard him raise his voice,' Saif confided as he strode out of the room next door.

'I'm not scared of him and he no longer has any influence with me,' Tati admitted tightly, very pale, her blue eyes shadowed. 'But it was very unpleasant. He was shocked at what I had to tell him. Even after what he did, he still thought he could talk me into giving him the Fosters Manor estate, but I refused him and told him that when the time came I will be signing the London apartment over to Ana, so that she will still have a home. If she chooses to have her parents live with her there that's their business, not mine. I will warn her that her father is likely to try to persuade her to put the apartment in his name and that she must not agree to that. I can do no more. I understand that my uncle is likely to get a prison sentence of short duration as he has no previous record and that my aunt is likely to get community work. So, that's it now, all done and dusted.'

'You're exhausted,' Saif pronounced, bending down and scooping her bodily out of her chair before she could even guess what he was planning to do.

'I don't know why,' she sighed as he carried her through to the bedroom and settled her down on the bed.

'You're pregnant and the stress hasn't helped. Dr Abaza said that you would probably be unusually tired these first weeks.'

Tati got ready for bed, wondering if Saif would be joining her, because there was another bedroom available. She was thinking that it was far too early for him to even be thinking of sleeping and recalling that the night before he had not come to bed at all when her own eyes drifted shut.

In the morning, she felt strong enough to deal with just about anything. Even leaving Saif? She studied him over breakfast, a clenching low down in her belly as she collided with those spectacular eyes of his, hunger flaming through her in warning. Heat built in her cheeks and flushed through her entire body and she pressed her thighs together, thinking that Saif still mesmerised her. Swearing off him, taking a step back, was horrendously difficult when every natural impulse drew her back to him.

'You're coming down to the manor with me?' she queried in surprise. 'I thought you had work to do.'

'The work is always there. If I didn't ignore it sometimes I would never have any free time at all,' Saif asserted with a flashing smile that was none-theless distinctly tense to her gaze.

He couldn't actually have guessed what she was thinking about doing…could he? For goodness' sake, Tati scolded herself, he's not telepathic! And yet she couldn't escape the sneaking suspicion that somehow he knew, somehow he had worked out already that she had decided she could not continue their mar-riage on the basis he had suggested. It might be the sensible, kindest approach for their unborn child, but she was only human and neither a saint nor a mar-tyr and, if he pushed her, she would just tell him the truth so that he fully understood her position.

Tati dressed with care for the visit, donning a pretty polka-dot sundress that matched the sum-mer sky. As she had already discovered to her con-sternation, pregnancy changes had kicked into her body a lot sooner than she had expected and quite a few items no longer fitted comfortably. Her breasts had swelled while her waist seemed to be vanishing. Luckily, a looser dress hid the fact.

Saif watched his wife's shuttered face begin to light up as they turned into the driveway of the old house. She was happy coming back here, happy that she was going to leave him. He straightened his wide shoulders and breathed in deep as they approached the front door, and she began to dig in her bag for the keys her uncle had handed over.

'Use the doorbell. When I realised you were coming here, I had cleaners and a housekeeper hired to greet you,' Saif divulged stiffly.

'Good grief, why would you do that?' Tati exclaimed, discomfiture claiming her afresh.

'You will not be a servant in your own home,' Saif breathed thinly.

'I'm pregnant, not disabled!' Tati protested. 'I'm not like Ana. I'm very self-sufficient. I can cook, clean, do *anything*.'

'But you will not…today anyway,' Saif completed flatly.

A pleasant older woman welcomed them into the wainscoted hall. It shone with cleanliness and the scent of beeswax polish was in the air. Tati smiled, recalling it that way from her childhood. Wandering into the pretty but faded drawing room, she went straight to the piano to study the photos there, picking up one of her grandparents when they had still been hale and hearty. She wasn't remotely surprised that, while there were a few gaps where her uncle and aunt had removed their own pieces of furniture, they had left behind all the family photos.

Two little blonde girls were in the background of the picture, giggling, and beside them stood a tall, elegant blonde with a bright smile. 'Ana and me,' she told Saif. 'And that's my mother with us.'

Her eyes throbbed and her throat ached as she thought back to those days at the manor before her uncle took over.

'I won't let you leave me!' Saif breathed with startling abruptness into the silence.

In consternation, Tati spun round to look at him, her face as red as fire because he *had* guessed what she was planning. 'You make it sound so emotional when it's not,' she muttered uncomfortably. 'I don't know how you guessed that I was thinking of living here and of not returning to Alharia with you.'

Saif lifted his strong jaw, green eyes glittering. 'I know you and I won't let you do it.'

Regret softened her blue eyes. 'I'm afraid I don't see how you can stop me.'

'I'd kidnap you,' Saif announced, disconcerting her so completely that she simply stared at him with a dropped jaw. 'Maybe after the baby was born. I wouldn't want you harmed by the exercise... obviously.'

But there was nothing remotely obvious in that threat that Tati could understand. She adored him but there was no denying that he was a conventional guy, occasionally even rather strait-laced. Remarkably handsome and sexy and full of charisma, but not the sort who broke rules. Hadn't she watched him freeze before her very eyes when Ana had tried to flirt with him? He had been appalled and he hadn't known how to handle it without being rude. So, for Saif to talk about kidnapping her with apparent seriousness shocked her beyond bearing.

'You wouldn't do anything like that,' she told him gently. 'It just wouldn't be your style.'

'If I am forced to live without you, I can make it my style,' Saif assured her with perfect gravity.

Tati sighed with regret. 'Look, you said a lot of true, logical things when we talked. Yes, it would be better for our child if we stayed together for the first years, but I just can't face a future where I'd be living a lie.'

'I will do whatever it takes to keep you…even if I have to change myself. I will change for you,' Saif swore with sincerity.

Her eyes stung with tears. 'You don't need to change. It's *me* who has the problem. I broke our rules: I fell in love with you…and I want much *more* from you than a fake marriage, and that's unfair to you.'

'You…you love me?' Saif almost whispered, staring at her fixedly as if that were the biggest shock he had ever had.

'I wouldn't have told you if you hadn't been talking that…er…weird way,' she muttered in mortification.

'Weird?' Saif's mouth quirked. 'As in being willing to consider kidnapping you? Doesn't it occur to you that while you were falling in love I might have been too?'

Her blue eyes widened, and she shifted infinitesimally closer to his tall, muscular frame. 'Might you have been?'

'First time I've ever been in love. First and last time,' Saif intoned hoarsely, curving a not-quite-steady hand to the curve of her cheekbone. 'I want you in my life for ever and ever like the stupid fairy tales.'

'Fairy tales are not stupid,' Tati told him tenderly, happiness surging up through her in an ungovernable flood. 'How come I'm your first love? There *must* have been someone else at some stage.'

'Maybe I was a late developer,' Saif quipped. 'I was always very careful not to spend too much time with any woman because I feared falling for someone I couldn't have. I knew that eventually my father would expect me to marry a woman of his choice.'

That caution was so much in his nature that she almost laughed. She turned her head to see the new housekeeper in the doorway offering them coffee. 'That would be lovely but…perhaps, later,' she suggested. 'I want to show my husband round the house first.'

'I suppose we should take a look at the outside first,' Saif remarked levelly.

'No, we're heading for the nearest bedroom,' Tati whispered, amused by his innocence. 'I'm about to jump your bones like a wild, wanton woman.'

'With you, wild and wanton works very well for me,' Saif murmured with a sudden laugh of appreciation. 'I'm more relaxed with you than I have ever been with a woman. I suppose we'll be stuck with visits from your ghastly cousin, Ana, for ever.'

'No, she won't be flirting with you the next time we see her. You withstood her attractions and that hurts her ego and turns her off. Next time, she'll be telling me that she doesn't know how I stand you being so quiet... She doesn't realise that you were only quiet because she embarrassed you,' Tati commented cheerfully.

'I wasn't embarrassed,' Saif contradicted. 'I just don't like women who are all over me like a rash.'

'Like me?' Tati teased, stretching up on tiptoe to kiss him, her hands roaming across his chest beneath his jacket as she pressed into his lean, strong length in an act of deliberate provocation.

'You're the sole exception,' Saif husked as she linked her fingers with his and urged him towards the stairs. 'Would you really have stayed here and left me?'

'If you hadn't said you loved me, I think…yes,' she muttered guiltily. 'I would have been so unhappy believing that you were only tolerating me until you felt it was time for us to split up.'

'I tolerate you with pleasure…that doesn't sound quite right,' Saif husked on the landing as he bent over her, nibbling a caressing trail down the slope of her neck. 'We need a bed.'

'I'm not sure there'll be one made up.'

'I ordered a new bed for the main bedroom and said we would be staying the night.'

Tati gazed up at him, impressed to death by that level of preparation. 'How did you know we'd be here for the night?'

'You've been so distant since we had that discussion at the palace that I knew I was in trouble,' Saif confided. 'I was determined to persuade you to stay with me…*somehow*. But I didn't know how I was going to do it, only that I would need a good few hours to have a chance of accomplishing it.'

'You're so modest,' Tati muttered, tugging him into the main bedroom, relieved to see that, aside from the new bed and bedding, it looked much as it had in her grandparents' day. Thankfully, her uncle and aunt had removed every shred of their presence. 'I can't believe we are here in this house together and that you love me.'

'Believe,' he urged fiercely as he flipped off her shoes and unzipped her dress, lifting her to arrange

her on the bed like a precious sacrifice. 'I love you so much. You have no idea how it felt to think that I was losing you for ever…and all because I said the wrong things.'

'It took you a while to realise how you felt,' Tati told him forgivingly, stroking a fingertip across one high cheekbone.

'No, it didn't. I started suspecting way back when I kissed you in the street after we got off that Ferris wheel in the Place de la Concorde. I've never done anything like that in my adult life, but I couldn't resist you when you smiled. I knew then that I'd never felt that way in my life…it was *so* powerful,' he admitted. 'But I refused to examine my emotions because it didn't fit in with our plans and I was afraid that you would walk away the way my mother once walked away from me.'

Tati groaned and wrapped her arms round him tightly, touched to the heart. 'I'm not walking away. I'm never going anywhere. Gosh, you were a pushover. It took me much longer because I was working hard at trying not to get attached to you. Trouble is…' she sighed blissfully, sitting up helpfully to make the removal of her bra easier '…you're an attachable guy.'

Saif chuckled. 'You just made up a word. What does it mean?'

Her fingertip traced the sensual line of his lower lip. 'It means that there's a whole lot of stuff I like about you…like how protective you are. I've never had that before and at first I confused that protectiveness with you trying to boss me around, and I'd suffered way too much of that kind of treatment here.'

'You start shouting when I try to boss you around,' Saif pointed out with unholy amusement gleaming in his stunning eyes. 'I like your feistiness and your lack of guile and greed and also…your generosity. I still want to lock your uncle and aunt up and starve and torture them for the way they mistreated you, but I admire and respect your compassion.'

'They're already losing everything they value… the house, the money, the lifestyle, their reputations. That's enough of a punishment, but I will have to watch out that they don't take advantage of Ana.'

Saif winced. 'That will be a lifelong challenge.'

'But I can do it,' she told him gently while pushing him flat and unbuttoning his shirt, spreading appreciative hands over his bronzed hair-roughened skin and lingering with a boldness she had never dared to utilise with him before. 'I'm feeling much more confident since I met you…'

Saif gave her a wicked grin. 'I am more than willing to lie back and think only of the greatness of Alharia for your benefit, *aziz*.'

'I can't believe it only took you a couple of days to start falling in love with me,' she told him happily.

'You're a class act,' Saif husked, winding long fingers into her rumpled blond hair, the warmth and tenderness in his gaze like a sublime caress on her skin. 'An act no other woman will ever match.'

'I think you're pretty special too,' she whispered against the marauding mouth circling hers with unhidden hunger, and then they both forgot to talk and got entirely carried away into their own little world of mutual satisfaction and happiness.

EPILOGUE

Five years later

SAIF GLANCED ACROSS the room to where his wife was seated beside his father. It was the Emir's birthday. He was ninety years old and just months earlier had stepped down from the throne to allow his son to become Regent. Freed from the stress of ruling, the older man had become much more relaxed, in a way his son had never expected to see.

Their children—Amir, who was four, and the toddler twins, Farah and Milly—were playing at the Emir's feet, absorbed in the latest toys he had presented them with. For the first time ever, Saif reflected fondly, his father was enjoying a peaceful family atmosphere and he owed that blessing to Tatiana.

His father adored his daughter-in-law. He was fond of telling people that his own life would have been very different had he had the good fortune to meet a Tatiana. As to his pride in having married his son off to the grandchild of his old friend, that went without saying. But the knowledge that his father was happy and at peace and delighted in his grandchildren made Saif's duties a lot easier.

The Emir had not changed personality overnight, but he had become less authoritarian and more willing to listen to other points of view. On the other side of the room his three older sisters, engaged in their endless embroidery and crochet, were chattering to Tatiana, smiling and laughing, patting the slight swell of her stomach affectionately.

Thanks to his rashness, their fourth child was due in a handful of months, Saif mused ruefully. Strange how he had never had a reckless bone in his body until Tatiana came along, but then he had also never been happier. When Tatiana had learned that she was carrying twins the last time, they had decided that three children were enough, and then Tatiana's amazing fertility had collided with his desire to have sex in their private pool and the result was before them. He smiled abstractedly as he watched his beautiful wife weaving her magic with his family. The pool encounter had been spectacularly worthwhile.

As Tati's mobile phone buzzed she excused herself and walked through an open archway out to a terrace to take her call. The Emir had not noticed the phone ringing and she was relieved. While the old man was a lot less grumpy than he had once been, he still held on to many of what his son deemed to be 'medieval prejudices.'

'George wants a baby,' Ana proclaimed in a tragic voice.

'Well, you knew it was on the cards,' Tati reminded her cousin, who had been married for four years. George had finally proposed and stuck to his word after Ana began seeing another man. A banker, George Davis-Appleton was a clever character, more than equal to the task of keeping his avaricious in-laws at bay, and that had meant that Tati could finally relax and know her cousin was safe from exploitation.

'You love my kids…why shouldn't you love your own child?' Tati asked cheerfully.

'It's not that, Tati.' Ana sighed. 'But when you have a baby you have to grow up and I'm not ready for that yet.'

'But George is, so you have to consider him as well. Look, it's the Emir's birthday party here, so I can't talk for long,' Tati warned her cousin, soothing Ana's fears about motherhood aging her overnight.

Rupert and Elizabeth Hamilton had both received prison sentences after the crooked solicitor had declared that her aunt had been present at his meetings with his client. Within eighteen months, however, both of them had been released and they had moved in with their daughter. With Ana married, they still lived there, and Tati hadn't seen her uncle since their last meeting at the hotel, a situation that she was quite content with.

Saif and Tati regularly stayed at the manor when they were in England and spent every Christmas there. Her mother's cousin, Pauline, had moved in as a sort of caretaker for the property when it was empty. Tati's life had changed radically but very much for the better, she conceded cheerfully, because she was fiercely content and happy with Saif and their family.

She glanced up and saw her husband watching her from the archway.

'Hi,' she murmured softly, blue eyes locking to him, brimming with love and appreciation. Tall, dark and devastatingly handsome, he still rocked her where she stood every time she looked at him.

He closed his arms round her slowly. 'You look tired.'

'It was exhausting trying to explain Father Christmas to your father…because there isn't really an explanation and he doesn't like fanciful stuff.'

'It's what you call an own goal, *aziz*. You persuaded him to join us in England for Christmas this year. He wants to be prepared for some weird old man in a red suit trying to squeeze himself down a chimney…' Saif laughed softly.

Tati mock-punched a broad shoulder. 'Don't you dare tell Amir that version. He's already very excited about Christmas.'

'Relax. It's still summer,' Saif reminded her, bending his dark glossy head to steal a kiss from her soft pink lips and a little flame ignited low in her pelvis, provoking a moan deep in her throat.

His mouth circled and teased hers and she squirmed against him, helpless in the grip of that hunger as he backed her up against the wall edging the terrace, ultimately dragging his lips from hers with a groan. 'We can't leave until my father retires for the night,' he reminded her hoarsely.

Tati chuckled and bumped her brow in reproach against his shoulder before stepping back from him. 'You're like oil on a bonfire for me... I'm not complaining,' she murmured with reddening cheeks as she smiled up at him with adoring eyes that he cherished. 'I love you so much.'

Their little private moment was invaded by clattering feet and noisy voices. Amir pelted out with his two-year-old sisters hard in his wake, shouting at him to wait for them. He was tall and black-haired like Saif with the same wonderful green eyes. Farah and Milly were an identical mix of blond-haired blue-eyed little girls with pale golden skin and as lively as Amir was steady like his father.

Saif hoisted up his daughters in his strong arms and walked back indoors. Amir's hand slid into his mother's and he yawned. 'I was trying to tell Grandpa about Father Christmas, but he got all mixed up,' he complained.

As Saif's keen gaze encountered Tati's, he was smiling, warmth and tenderness a vibrant presence in that appraisal, and happiness that was as solid as gold shimmered through her. She had everything she had ever wanted in life.

* * * * *

Head over heels for
Cinderella's Desert Baby Bombshell?
Don't forget to catch the next instalment in the Heirs for Royal Brothers duet!

Also, don't miss these other Lynne Graham stories.

The Italian in Need of an Heir
A Baby on the Greek's Doorstep
Christmas Babies for the Italian
The Greek's Convenient Cinderella
The Ring the Spaniard Gave Her

Available now!

WE HOPE YOU ENJOYED
THIS BOOK FROM
HARLEQUIN
PRESENTS

Escape to exotic locations where passion knows no bounds.

Welcome to the glamorous lives of royals and billionaires, where passion knows no bounds. Be swept into a world of luxury, wealth and exotic locations.

8 NEW BOOKS AVAILABLE EVERY MONTH!

#3945 HER BEST KEPT ROYAL SECRET
Heirs for Royal Brothers
by Lynne Graham

Independent Gaby thought nothing could be more life-changing than waking up in the bed of the playboy prince who was so dangerous to her heart... Until she's standing in front of Angel a year later, sharing her shocking secret—his son!

#3946 CROWNED FOR HIS DESERT TWINS
by Clare Connelly

To become king, Sheikh Khalil must marry...immediately. But first, a mind-blowing whirlwind night with India McCarthy that neither can resist! When India reveals she's pregnant, can a ring secure his crown...and his heirs?

#3947 FORBIDDEN TO HER SPANISH BOSS
The Acostas!
by Susan Stephens

Rose Kelly can't afford any distractions. Especially her devilishly attractive boss, Raffa Acosta! But a week of networking on his superyacht may take them from professional to dangerously passionate territory...

#3948 SHY INNOCENT IN THE SPOTLIGHT
The Scandalous Campbell Sisters
by Melanie Milburne

Elspeth's sheltered existence means she's hesitant to swap places with her exuberant twin for a glamorous wedding. But the social spotlight is nothing compared to the laser focus of cynical billionaire Mack's undivided attention...

HPCNMRA0921

#3949 PROOF OF THEIR ONE HOT NIGHT
The Infamous Cabrera Brothers
by Emmy Grayson

One soul-stirring night with notorious tycoon Alejandro leaves Calandra pregnant. She plans to raise the baby alone. He's determined to prove he's parent material—and tempt her into another smoldering encounter...

#3950 HOW TO TEMPT THE OFF-LIMITS BILLIONAIRE
South Africa's Scandalous Billionaires
by Joss Wood

On a mission to acquire Roisin's South African vineyard, tycoon Muzi knows he needs to keep his eyes on the business deal, not his best friend's sister. Only, their forbidden temptation leads to even more forbidden nights...

#3951 THE ITALIAN'S BRIDE ON PAPER
by Kim Lawrence

When arrogant billionaire Samuele arrives at her door announcing his claim to her nephew, he sends Maya's senses into overdrive... She refuses to leave the baby's side, so he demands more—her as his convenient wife!

#3952 REDEEMED BY HIS NEW YORK CINDERELLA
by Jadesola James

Kitty will do anything for the foundation inspired by her tumultuous childhood. Even agree to a fake relationship to help Laurence, the impossibly guarded man from her past, land his next deal. Only, their chemistry is anything but make-believe!

YOU CAN FIND MORE INFORMATION ON UPCOMING HARLEQUIN TITLES, FREE EXCERPTS AND MORE AT HARLEQUIN.COM.